MAGICAL COCKTAILS
FOR WITCHES

MAGICAL Cocktails FOR Witches

80
ESSENTIAL RECIPES *for* LOVE, HEALTH, STRENGTH, *and* More

CAROLYN WNUK
CAROLINE PARADIS

Illustrations by JYOTIRMAYEE PATRA

ROCKRIDGE
PRESS

To our husbands, who have lovingly embraced
our ever-expanding witchiness.

Interior and Cover Designer: Jane Archer
Art Producer: Janice Ackerman
Editor: Anne Lowrey
Production Editor: Ashley Polikoff
Illustrations: ©2021 Jyotirmayee Patra

Paperback ISBN: 978-1-638-78038-0
eBook ISBN: 978-1-638-78289-6
R0

CONTENTS

INTRODUCTION vi

PART ONE: *The* CRAFT 1

Chapter 1:   MAGICAL MIXOLOGY 3

Chapter 2:   THROWING A SPELLBINDING
                     COCKTAIL PARTY 25

PART TWO: *Spiritual* LIBATIONS 35

Chapter 3:   LOVE & FRIENDSHIP 37

Chapter 4:   BEGINNINGS & ENDINGS 57

Chapter 5:   HEALTH & HEALING 77

Chapter 6:   CELEBRATIONS & SPIRITUAL GROWTH 97

Chapter 7:   STRENGTH & BOUNDARIES 117

MEASUREMENT CONVERSIONS 137

REFERENCES 138

INDEX 140

INTRODUCTION

Hello! We are Carolyn and Caroline. We met several years ago and became fast friends, often enjoying a craft cocktail while engaging in hours of conversation about energy work, past lives, crystals, and of course, witchcraft. Honestly, what's better than getting together with a woo friend and sipping on a delicious cocktail while contemplating life's most mystical questions?! (The answer is nothing.) Out of our love for magic, conversation, and mixology, the *Mystify Me* podcast was born. *Mystify Me* fuses our love for craft cocktails with our insatiable desire to explore unconventional, thought-provoking, new-age topics.

Among these mystical topics, witchcraft has a special place in our hearts. Through our spiritual journeys, we have both discovered that we deeply identify with witchcraft ideology and feel connected to the stories of the witch trials that have happened throughout history. We believe that witches are healers at heart, using Earth's resources to tap into their personal power, magic, and universal energy to heal themselves as well as their community. Through the podcast, we have become strong advocates for witchcraft, with a goal of demystifying what it means to be a witch. So, put down your pitchforks, people!

All jokes aside, our spiritual practices have taught us the power of infusing intention and magic into everyday activities. So, we thought, why not do it while making a cocktail? Cocktails are a fantastic vessel for spellcasting, intention setting, and personal healing. Now, we're not suggesting you guzzle 12 margaritas in a row—not much healing would come from that. However, the practice of gathering fresh ingredients provided by Mother Nature while calling upon their healing energies can be the perfect way to learn about witchcraft.

Not a witch? Not a mixologist? No problem! We will walk you through every step in this user-friendly guide. After a brief introduction, we'll fly into 80 exquisitely crafted cocktail recipes, organized by theme. We'll expand your capacity for love and strengthen the bonds of friendship in **chapter 3, Love & Friendship**. We then dive into **chapter 4, Beginnings & Endings**, so you can effortlessly let go of what's no longer serving you and celebrate new beginnings. **Chapter 5, Health & Healing**, takes you on a physical, emotional, and spiritual journey to help you heal on every level. Time to party with **chapter 6, Celebrations & Spiritual Growth**! Grab that sage stick, open that third eye, and create a space for celebration. And, finally, power up with **chapter 7, Strength & Boundaries**, as these powerful recipes and spells help you find courage, cut cords, and solidify boundaries.

We can't wait to get brewing with you! By the end of this book, you'll be the most badass witch on the block and the envy of your coven as you become a magical mixologist!

Disclaimer:

Okay, look—this is a cocktail book, not a doctor's visit. Although Carolyn and Caroline are both super knowledgeable and charming, the content in this book is NOT intended to be a substitute for professional medical advice, diagnosis, or treatment. Always seek the advice of your physician or other qualified healthcare provider with any questions you have regarding a medical or mental health condition. Also, Magical Cocktails for Witches's *content does not reflect the views of any professional organizations that Carolyn and Caroline are associated with. This book IS meant for entertainment, laughter, and personal/spiritual exploration—and to help you have fun dipping into mixology and the mystifying world around you.*

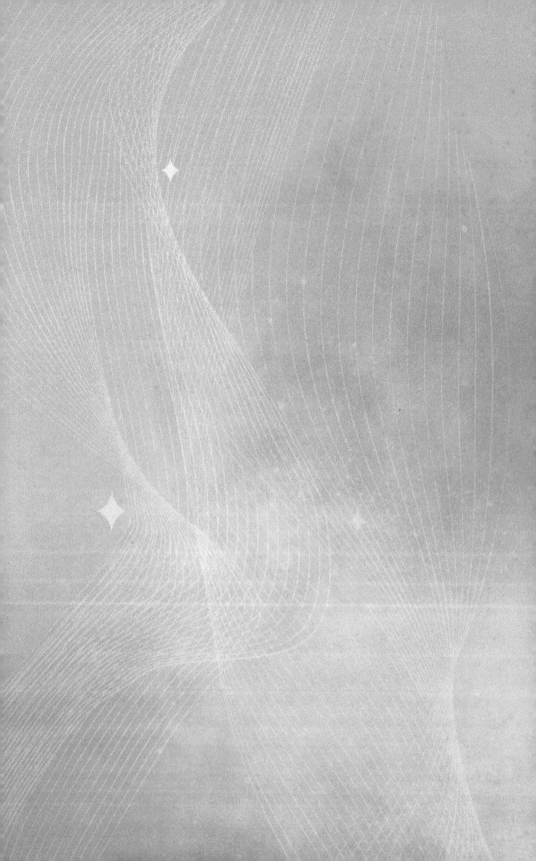

PART ONE

The CRAFT

You're about to learn everything you need to know to craft magical cocktails expertly! Let us guide you through potion brewing techniques as well as how to tap into your innate healing abilities through energy, intention, and spellcasting.

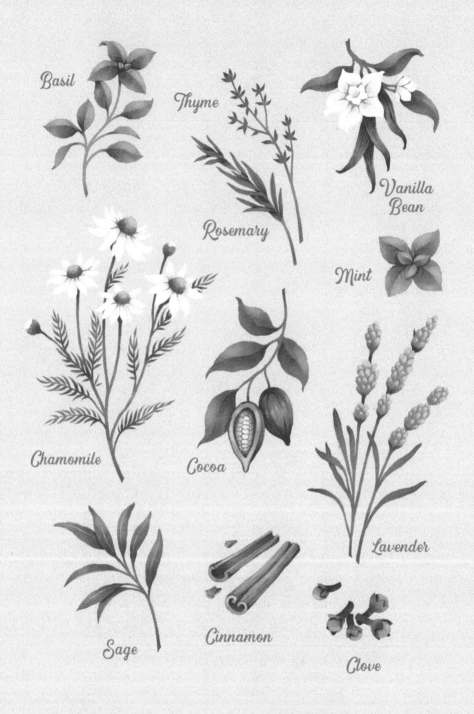

Basil

Thyme

Vanilla
Bean

Rosemary

Mint

Chamomile

Cocoa

Lavender

Sage

Cinnamon

Clove

1

MAGICAL MIXOLOGY

Welcome! We're going to kick-start this magical mixology journey by demystifying witchcraft *and* the process of cocktail creation. We'll also fly through essentials like drinkware, ingredients and garnishes, mixers, spirits, and tools, so you can confidently begin your brewing adventure.

What Is Witchcraft?

According to *Cunningham's Encyclopedia of Wicca in the Kitchen* by Scott Cunningham, witchcraft can be defined as: "The craft of a Witch; magic, especially magic utilizing personal power in conjunction with the energies, within food, stones, herbs, colors, and other natural objects." So, basically, witches practice nonthreatening, love-charged folk magic, using personal power and energies within natural objects to create needed change.

Developing a witchcraft practice is simpler than most people think. It's also highly individualized and marches to the beat of your drum. The witchcraft community encourages people to find their way by exploring resources, becoming familiar with foundational concepts, and gaining experience through practice.

Adding friends to the mix can make things even more magical. A coven is a group of people who practice witchcraft together with the goal of using the group's collective energy to magnify the potency of spells and rituals.

Cocktails the Witchy Way

A craft cocktail is a handmade alcoholic beverage, carefully and skillfully created using fresh ingredients. No premade mixers here—everything is made from scratch.

This book teaches you to create craft cocktails and become a mixologist, someone skilled at mixing cocktails and other drinks. But fair warning: If you get really good at this, your guests may never leave.

What separates this book from other cocktail recipe books is that we teach you how to not only make delicious cocktails but also cast spells and use specific ingredients to achieve desired outcomes, like manifesting abundance and increasing self-love. These cocktails become magical when you harness the energy of the ingredients by setting a positive intention for your goal.

The act of creating (or drinking) a handcrafted potion offers an opportunity to connect with others, including your coven, which enhances the collective energy. When multiple people consciously work on the same intention, the process can create a deeper impact on the material world.

Alcohol and Witchcraft

Throughout history in ancient civilizations, such as China, Egypt, Greece, and Rome, alcohol played an influential role. It was often used as a spiritual offering, a type of currency, and a component in religious and social ceremonies and celebrations. According to Julia Halina Hadas, author of *WitchCraft Cocktails*, alcohol has played an important role in witchcraft history as well. The use of alcohol was (and still is) a cornerstone of rituals and spellmaking.

Marysia Miernowska, author of *The Witch's Herbal Apothecary*, states that when combined with herbs, alcohol becomes a powerful conduit for extracting and magnifying Earth's healing properties. Alcohol also preserves the energetic and magical powers of botanicals for long-term use and storage. As such, alcohol is often a customary staple in any modern witch's home apothecary.

Tinctures, cocktails, and other concoctions transform into spells as soon as the witch infuses them with intention during creation. Therefore, the *intention* is the most powerful part of the spellmaking process. That said, it is completely acceptable for any witch to exclude alcohol from their spiritual or social practice. A witch's ability to harness the Universe's energy with intention does not hinge on the use of alcohol. As such, we include magical mocktail recipes that easily and effectively swap out alcohol for something else. Cheers, witches!

Mixing Cocktails and Brewing Potions

Brewing a potion typically involves preparing a beverage (like ale, coffee, or tea) by combining water and raw ingredients over heat. Mixing a cocktail uses a similar method, but instead of heat, mixologists commonly use ice. Whether mixing a cocktail or brewing a potion, both practices involve mindfully gathering ingredients, combining them skillfully, and extracting their physical and energetic qualities—whether for taste or mystical benefits.

Magic Mixology Words

The following mixology terms will enhance your understanding of cocktail fundamentals. Armed with this knowledge, you are well on your way to tackling magical and creative cocktails.

BLENDING: To mix cocktail ingredients with ice in a blender; commonly used to create frozen or blended drinks.

COCKTAIL: Alcohol and/or liqueurs combined with a mixer or modifier and often including bitters, syrups, and garnishes to add flavor and color.

DASH: A few drops, or a very small amount, of an ingredient.

LAYERING/FLOATING: A technique that creates a visually beautiful cocktail with color and flavor separation; pour the heavier alcohol into the glass first, then slowly pour the lighter alcohol over a spoon onto the heavier alcohol so that it floats on top.

MIXER: A nonalcoholic beverage, such as ginger beer, juice, soda, tonic, or water, mixed with alcohol to create a cocktail.

ROCKS (ON THE): Another word for ice; "on the rocks" means to pour the alcohol over ice to serve.

SHAKING: To fill a cocktail shaker tin (the bottom piece of a cocktail shaker) with ice, add the cocktail ingredients, cover with the tumbler (top piece), and shake for 10 to 18 seconds.

STIRRING: A gentler mixing technique than shaking; combine alcoholic ingredients and ice in a mixing glass, then stir with a bar spoon for at least 30 seconds.

STRAINING: Draining the liquid from the shaker or mixing glass.

Witchcraft Terms to Know

INTENTION: A wish or a desired outcome. Every thought we have affects the energy in our emotional, physical, and spiritual environment. Intentions are powerful in creating our reality and spellwork.

RITUAL: A practice performed with a specific intention and a desired outcome. Rituals are often community based, such as rites of passage, which involve coming together to harness the group's collective energy.

SPELL: Words spoken, out loud or in one's mind, for a desired outcome or intention. Spells are similar to prayers but are usually anchored by something physical, such as a candle, crystal, potion—or, in this case, a cocktail—which helps focus the spell's energy.

SPIRITUALLY SIGNIFICANT SPIRITS

Gin, with its juniper berry flavor, is an excellent choice for potions that focus on cleansing and protecting against negative energy or increasing abundance and prosperity.

Rum is the perfect partner for calling in abundance.

Vodka is a common and highly effective vehicle for making tinctures and bitters because of its high-proof distillation and neutral flavor. It's also a great preserver, maintaining the potent energies and healing properties of herbs without changing their scent or flavor.

Whiskey is another popular alcohol for making bitters and can be used in cocktails for ancestral work, positive change, or transformation.

Building Your Bar of Brews

Here are the essentials for creating the witchiest home bar ever, including options to keep costs down and still enjoy a bangin' bar! Use a cart, old bookshelf, or whatever strikes your fancy to hold your bar stock.

Drinkware

Presentation is everything—or is it? Yes, serving a cocktail in the correct glass can add to the experience, but witches were born to break rules! Whatever glass you're drawn to—or have on hand—will be perfect.

 COLLINS GLASS: This vessel holds 10 to 14 ounces and was named after the Tom Collins cocktail it is intended for! This glass is ideal for cocktails with high carbonation served over ice, as well as for tropical drinks, whether frozen or over ice.

 COUPE GLASS: Arguably, our favorite cocktail glass, thanks to the legend that it was molded from Marie Antoinette's left breast! The coupe glass is considered the ideal vessel for craft cocktails not served over ice, but it's also a fun option for margaritas and martinis.

 FLUTE GLASS: Use this fancy glass for Champagne, sparkling wine, or any cocktail that contains carbonation but no ice.

 IRISH COFFEE MUG: Designed to hold hot drinks, this cup is also great for magical teas.

 MARGARITA GLASS: This beautiful double-bowled coupe glass is famous for housing margaritas or any blended drink.

 MARTINI GLASS: This classic long-stemmed V-shaped glass is designed for the martini. However, as we said, witches march to their own drumbeat, so try a mudslide in this bad boy!

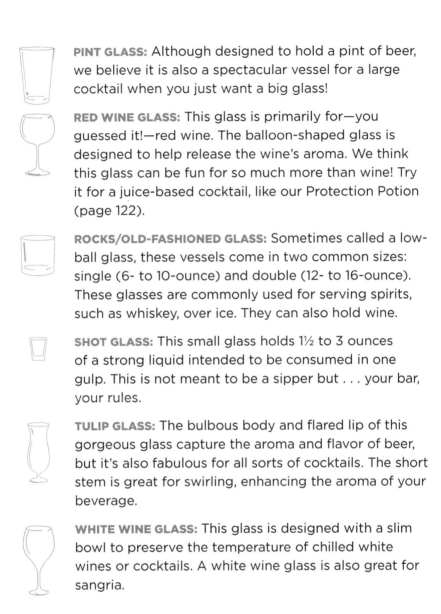

PINT GLASS: Although designed to hold a pint of beer, we believe it is also a spectacular vessel for a large cocktail when you just want a big glass!

RED WINE GLASS: This glass is primarily for—you guessed it!—red wine. The balloon-shaped glass is designed to help release the wine's aroma. We think this glass can be fun for so much more than wine! Try it for a juice-based cocktail, like our Protection Potion (page 122).

ROCKS/OLD-FASHIONED GLASS: Sometimes called a low-ball glass, these vessels come in two common sizes: single (6- to 10-ounce) and double (12- to 16-ounce). These glasses are commonly used for serving spirits, such as whiskey, over ice. They can also hold wine.

SHOT GLASS: This small glass holds 1½ to 3 ounces of a strong liquid intended to be consumed in one gulp. This is not meant to be a sipper but . . . your bar, your rules.

TULIP GLASS: The bulbous body and flared lip of this gorgeous glass capture the aroma and flavor of beer, but it's also fabulous for all sorts of cocktails. The short stem is great for swirling, enhancing the aroma of your beverage.

WHITE WINE GLASS: This glass is designed with a slim bowl to preserve the temperature of chilled white wines or cocktails. A white wine glass is also great for sangria.

Tools

When collecting these essential tools for your witchy bar, remember that you don't have to spend a lot of money! Many skilled mixologists and witches say the most important features of a tool are that it fits comfortably in your hand and is one you feel a bond with (such as your grandmother's measuring spoons).

BAR SPOON: A long spoon with a spiral handle and a small bowl at the end of a handle, used to stir drinks. You can also use a regular spoon.

BLENDER: Used to make blended cocktail ingredients, such as with spirits, fruit, and ice. Choose a countertop or handheld model or, in a pinch, a smoothie blender.

BOTTLE OPENER: Used to open bottles that do not have twist caps. The most important feature of a bottle opener is that it feels comfortable in your hand. There is no substitute for a bottle opener (please don't use your teeth).

CITRUS JUICER: This small kitchen tool extracts juice from citrus fruit. You can also use your hands!

COCKTAIL SHAKER: A mixing tool, usually made from metal, in which cocktail ingredients and ice are combined, then shaken, using a mixing glass to create the seal. If you do not have a cocktail shaker, hold two pint-size glasses together tightly, and shake (ideally, over the sink and to the rhythm of a sweet beat).

COCKTAIL SPEARS: Made from metal, plastic, or wood and used as a decorative element to spear fruit, olives, and other cocktail garnishes. Toothpicks are a great substitute.

CORKSCREW: A tool used to open and remove corks, typically from wine bottles.

FINE-MESH SIEVE: This kitchen tool helps remove seeds, muddled fruit, and herbs from drinks. Straining through cheesecloth also works.

HAWTHORNE STRAINER: This metal bar tool, which fits into any cocktail shaker, features a metal spiral around the front edge and is used to strain cocktails. If you don't have one, use a fine-mesh sieve.

JIGGER: This double-ended, hourglass-shaped, steel measuring tool measures liquids. The smaller side measures ¾ ounce and the larger side measures 1½ ounces. A shot glass can be used in place of a jigger, which also measures 1½ ounces.

MEASURING SPOONS: Used to measure specific amounts of wet or dry ingredients.

MORTAR AND PESTLE: Used to mash (muddle) fresh fruits, herbs, or spices to release their essential oils, aroma, and flavor. A wooden spoon or fork can be a substitute.

MUDDLER: A bar tool used to muddle fresh fruits and spices.

PARING KNIFE: A small knife used for peeling and cutting fruit and other ingredients, such as herbs.

VEGETABLE PEELER: The main tool used for creating citrus twists and garnishes. You can also accomplish this with a knife, but use caution. Your drink won't taste as good if you're missing a finger.

ZESTER: A metal tool used for obtaining the zest from citrus fruits. You can also use a box grater or, in a pinch, a paring knife.

Spirits

We've identified the spirits needed for the recipes in this book—don't feel like you must buy them all at once! Start with a few recipes that speak to you, then build your bar at your own pace.

BOURBON: With its strong notes of caramel, oak, and vanilla, bourbon is sweeter than other types of whiskey. It's often enjoyed neat or on the rocks but can also make a great cocktail. Maker's Mark is a classic option that won't break the bank.

BRANDY/COGNAC: Brandy is a distilled spirit made from fermented fruit juice, typically yielding a taste of flowers, fruit, or citrus. There are many types of brandy but Cognac is considered the most popular. In order for a brandy to be classified as Cognac, it must be made with grapes from the Cognac region of France.

CREAM LIQUEURS: A liqueur made with cream, such as Baileys Irish Cream. Baileys features a sweet milk-chocolatey flavor with a whiskey base, cream, and cocoa extract.

FRUIT AND NUT LIQUEURS: These alcoholic drinks are flavored with fruit, herbs, or nuts and are enjoyed neat or on the rocks. We use Amaretto, coffee liqueur, crème de menthe, elderflower liqueur, pumpkin liqueur, and triple sec.

GIN: The juniper berry gives gin, the key ingredient of a classic martini, its trademark pine flavor. Aviation and Bombay Sapphire are our go-tos.

GREEN CHARTREUSE: This sweet, spicy, smooth-flavored liqueur is known for its distinctly herbal finish.

RUM: Made from sugar cane, rum can be found in light (white) and dark varieties and features strong vanilla, caramel, and toasted oak flavors. Bacardi is a must-have for any home bar.

SCHNAPPS: Schnapps is a type of distilled spirit. Common flavors are peach and peppermint.

SPARKLING WINE: Molecules of carbon dioxide gas create the characteristic bubbles. Champagne, prosecco, and sparkling rosé are popular options.

TEQUILA: Tequila is made from the blue agave plant, giving it a smooth, earthy flavor with a slightly sweet undertone. Like rum, tequila is found in both light and dark varieties. Camarena or Espolòn are good choices.

VODKA: Equally adept at delivering a savory martini as well as a fruity frozen cocktail, we consider vodka the breakout star of the home bar. Ketel One and Tito's vodka are tasty, affordable options.

WHISKEY: This distilled spirit is typically aged in a barrel, making it different from other spirits, such as vodka. Varieties include bourbon, Irish whiskey, rye, and Scotch, as well as specialty flavors like peanut butter whiskey and banana whiskey, which add fun flavor to cocktails. WhistlePig and Basil Hayden are low in price but high in taste.

Mixers and Infusions

Let's mix it up! You'll find lots of mixers and infusions at local liquor/package stores and your grocery store. Check our list for staple suggestions to stock your home bar.

COLA: Made from kola nut extract, which brings energy, peace, and a sense of calm. Cola is typically paired with rum.

CRANBERRY JUICE: Energetically associated with abundance, health, love, and protection.

GINGER ALE: Flavored with ginger extract, ginger invokes good health, love, protection, sensuality, and success.

GINGER BEER: Flavored with ginger, which can alleviate nausea and improve digestion.

GRENADINE: Made from pomegranate juice, sugar, and lemon juice; used for wisdom and fertility magic.

HERBAL TEA: A type of infusion; a beverage made from dried plant matter steeped in hot water, offering an array of health benefits. Our favorite teas are chamomile, green, hibiscus, lavender, and lemon balm.

HOT SAUCE / CHILI POWDER / CAYENNE PEPPER: Made from chiles, these ingredients add the element of fire.

LEMON JUICE: Contains powerful cleansing and purification qualities to help remove negative energy or blockages and opens a channel for spiritual connection.

LIME JUICE: Increases energetic protection against negative energy and repels any ill will.

PINEAPPLE JUICE: Adds a splash for good fortune and luck.

PUMPKIN PUREE: Supports fertility, granting wishes, love, prosperity, and protection.

SIMPLE SYRUPS: Made by dissolving sugar in water, simple syrups add sweetness. Making these from scratch, especially when adding herbs and spices, is a great way to add complex flavor to cocktails (see page 20).

SPARKLING WATER: Carbonated water, such as soda water and club soda.

TOMATO JUICE: Great for attracting or increasing love and passion and protecting from negative influences.

TONIC WATER: A carbonated soft drink made with quinine.

WATERMELON PUREE: Releases heavy emotions and lust, clears energy blocks, and provides all-purpose healing and emotional release when you need to move on.

✦✦ THE ICE ELEMENT ✦✦

The function of ice in a cocktail is to lower the temperature of the drink and to add water and/or texture; its importance in a craft cocktail cannot be overstated. There are five types of ice: cubes, crescent, flake, gourmet, and nugget.

It's important to note that the water from the ice affects flavor as it dilutes the cocktail: too much water means the cocktail becomes diluted and tastes weak; too little, and the cocktail tastes strong and the alcohol could create a warm or burning sensation. Consider the shape and size of your cubes as you create your drink. Large cubes, like whiskey cubes, melt more slowly than smaller ones, such as crushed ice.

Garnishes

Garnishes not only add style, flair, and pizazz to your cocktails but also produce a more potent potion, magnifying the intention of your magical creation. They can be placed on the rim of the glass, dropped into the cocktail, sprinkled on top, or speared with a cocktail spear. Here are our favorite garnishes, their magical qualities, and how to display them on (and in) your cocktail creations.

BASIL: Abundance, courage, love, luck, prosperity, protection, trust; enhances mental abilities; a sprig is dropped into the drink.

BERRIES: Antioxidants and anti-inflammatory benefits; dropped whole into the drink or skewered on a cocktail spear and placed into the cocktail or on the glass rim.

CHAMOMILE: Soothes anxiety, reduces stress, and supports restful sleep and healing; transforms bad luck; sprinkled on top.

CHERRY: Fertility and love; dropped into a drink.

CINNAMON: Healing, love, lust, money, protection, psychic awareness, purification, success; ground cinnamon is sprinkled on top; whole sticks are placed in the glass.

CLOVE: Attraction, comfort, enhanced mental abilities, protection, purification; ground clove is sprinkled on top; whole cloves are dropped into the glass.

COCOA POWDER / CHOCOLATE: General well-being, love; sprinkled or shaved into a drink.

Lavender

LAVENDER: Happiness, healing, love, peace, wisdom; sprinkled on top.

LEMON: Love and happiness; cleansing, protection, purification; sliced and placed on the rim of the glass or floated on top; a twist of peel is dropped into the drink.

Olive

LIME: Love, luck, purification; enhances sleep; sliced and placed on the rim of the glass or floated on top; a twist of peel is dropped into the drink.

MINT: Health, love, mental clarity, money, purification, success; a sprig is dropped into the drink.

OLIVES: Friendship, peace, victory—plus loads of health benefits; skewered on a cocktail spear and placed into the cocktail or on the glass rim.

ORANGE: Joy, love, prosperity, purification; sliced and placed on the rim of the glass or floated on top; a twist of peel is dropped into the drink.

POMEGRANATE SEEDS: Wisdom, patience, communication with others; floated on the drink.

ROSE: Psychic ability; manifests good fortune, healing, love, self-love; petals are floated on top.

ROSEMARY: Cleansing, healing, longevity, protection; a sprig is dropped into the drink.

SAGE: Cleanses negative energy; good health, healing, longevity, protection, psychic awareness; a sprig is dropped into the drink.

THYME: Courage, divination, healing, psychic cleansing, purification; enhances memory, eases sleep; a sprig is dropped into the drink.

VANILLA BEAN: Purification; restoring and enhancing energy, strengthening mental abilities; laid on the glass rim or placed into the drink.

✦✦ THE POWER OF BITTERS ✦ ✦

Bitters is a spirit infused with plant matter, so it takes on a bitter to bittersweet flavor. Many cocktails have primary flavors of sweet or sour, so a bit of bitters adds complexity with just a few drops.

Did you know that bitters also hold a strong connection to witchcraft? In witchcraft's early days, healers had difficulty growing or procuring fresh healing herbs and plants based on seasonal availability. Storing plants for long periods was an equally challenging issue. To solve these problems, witches and healers made tinctures and bitters from these ingredients for long-term storage and year-round use.

Brewing Your Magic Potion

Time to get movin' and shakin'! These potion brewing techniques will bring your magical beverages to life.

CALLING UPON MAGIC: Each ingredient has unique energetic healing properties. For example, basil's properties are of love, prosperity, and trust. To call upon basil's love properties for a love spell, place the herb in your hand, and say, "I invoke basil's magical ability to bring more love into my life."

CENTERING AND GROUNDING YOURSELF: Stand or sit with your feet on the floor. Take a couple of deep breaths, feel the earth supporting and grounding you, and bring your awareness to your breath as it moves through your body.

INFUSING INTENTION: With your desired goal clarified, create a positive affirmation. Speak these words as if they are true. For example, "I am loved. Love flows easily and effortlessly into my life."

PREPARING YOUR SPACE: It's a good practice to cleanse your physical and energetic spaces. The most common way is smoke cleansing, which is done by burning a sage stick or piece of palo santo.

VISUALIZATION: This technique, using your mind's eye (imagination) to create an image of what you want to call in, can help you focus your intention while performing your spell or ritual.

Mint

✦ ALL WITCHES WELCOME: MAKING A MOCKTAIL ✦

Although spirits are the base ingredient for the recipes in this book, they are by no means a necessity. It's easy to put a non-alcoholic spin on any of our concoctions!

Bubble up: Add sparkling water to give your beverage extra pizzazz. We especially love using a flavored seltzer!

Fake it 'til you make it: Add a teaspoon or two of pickle juice or caper juice to your cocktail to mimic the taste of alcohol! Sounds crazy, we know, but trust us!

Make it pretty: Create a feast for the eyes, and the taste buds will follow! Fancy up that drink with a stunning glass, lots of ice, a splash of cranberry juice for color, and a gorgeous garnish.

Crafting a Cocktail

This is the exciting part, building the cocktail. With these six steps, you can create any magical craft cocktail.

STEP 1: Prepare your space, center and ground yourself, and set your intention.

STEP 2: Gather your tools and ingredients, and call upon them to unleash their magical potential.

STEP 3: Do the prep, such as muddling ingredients, chilling your glass, making simple syrup, and preparing garnishes.

STEP 4: Build your cocktail, starting with the base spirit. Add mixers, liqueurs, bitters, and any other ingredients.

STEP 5: Pour the cocktail into your glass (over ice, if called for). Top with a carbonated beverage (if called for) last to preserve the bubbles and avoid any potential explosions from shaking.

STEP 6: Garnish, give thanks for this experience, proceed with the spell, and enjoy your cocktail!

Incorporating Rituals and Spells

This ain't your grandma's cocktail book (unless she's a witch, in which case she will be totally down with this). Each recipe is paired with a ritual or spell that can be performed individually or shared with friends (your coven).

+ Have fun, and open your mind—don't worry about doing everything perfectly or abiding by any rules.

+ Be in the right mind-set! Give yourself 30 minutes after work to decompress before you start a spell.

+ Call in your spirit posse, including angels, animal spirits, loved ones who have passed on, spirit guides, or a bevy of other positive beings to support you during any spiritual work. Say something like, "I call upon my spirit posse to guide, support, and protect me during this ritual. May the outcome be according to my highest healing good."

Potion-Making Tips

It's a hard and fast rule that witches are unique individuals, so often the best spells are the ones that are created by the witch that performs them. Let your intuition guide you! Consider this your free pass to go rogue and run wild! When creating a craft cocktail, you may find that you connect to the potion more when you use the ingredients and tools that most resonate with you.

Naming your creation will bring it to life! Here are a few questions to ask yourself when naming your cocktail: What kinds of feelings does it conjure up when you're drinking it? What ingredients are being used? What are the energetic properties of those ingredients? Again, there's no wrong way to do this!

✦ CRAFTING SIMPLE SYRUPS ✦

These handcrafted simple syrups are key components in our cocktail recipes. Making these syrups adds steps, but they're easy, and the results are worth it!

For each, in a small saucepan, combine the ingredients, and cook over medium heat, stirring, until the sugar dissolves. Remove from the heat, and let cool. Refrigerate covered for 1 to 2 weeks.

Classic Simple Syrup:
1 cup water + 1 cup sugar

Blackberry Simple Syrup:
1 cup chopped fresh blackberries + 1 cup water + 1 cup sugar

Cinnamon-Rosemary Simple Syrup:
5 cinnamon sticks + 2 large rosemary sprigs +
1 cup water + 1 cup sugar

Honey-Lavender Simple Syrup:
½ cup honey + ½ cup water +
2 tablespoons dried culinary-grade lavender

Mint Simple Syrup:
15 fresh mint leaves + 1 cup water + 1 cup sugar

Strawberry Simple Syrup:
4 fresh strawberries, muddled + ½ cup water + ¼ cup sugar

Vanilla Bean Simple Syrup:
1 fresh vanilla bean, split + 1 cup water + 1 cup sugar

Magical Flourishes

Let's finish this drink with style! In addition to the garnishes discussed on page 14, a final flourish is like the touch of your magic wand.

CITRUS TWIST: Using a vegetable peeler, peel a thin, straight strip of citrus about 2 inches long, then twist into a spiral shape. Spell: *I call upon the healing properties of this fruit to strengthen this drink's magical potency.*

FLAME A PEEL: This one gets a little wild! Have your cocktail ready. Using a vegetable peeler or paring knife, cut a thick piece of citrus peel. Hold the peel about 2 inches above the cocktail. Light a match, hold the peel close to the flame, and squeeze the oils from the peel. Poof! The oils will flame up and infuse your drink with aroma. Spell: *I call upon the element of fire to light my spiritual connection, ignite my intuition, and provide guidance in all things.*

WHEEL: Cut a citrus fruit in half crosswise. Slice the fruit crosswise into ¼-inch wheels. Spell: *As I create this wheel, I call upon my spirit posse to form a protective and nurturing circle to support me.*

Citrus

About the Recipes

Each recipe boasts a name and description of the magical and spiritual qualities of its ingredients, sprinkled with fun facts and witchy knowledge. We give you the ingredients, method, and tools needed. The spiritual cherry on top is the magical spell or ritual that can be performed to enhance your cocktail experience and to support your personal and spiritual growth.

Our cocktails are organized by theme, so you'll know exactly where to go based on your desired outcome. The recipes also include a label indicating the alcohol used, and each recipe offers a tip, such as:

BATCH IT: To make the cocktail in a large batch for a crowd.

MOCKTAIL MAGIC: To turn the cocktail into a mocktail.

SPELLBINDING SWAP: To swap out an ingredient for one that's more likely to be on hand.

In the next chapter, we'll explore how to throw a spellbinding cocktail party!

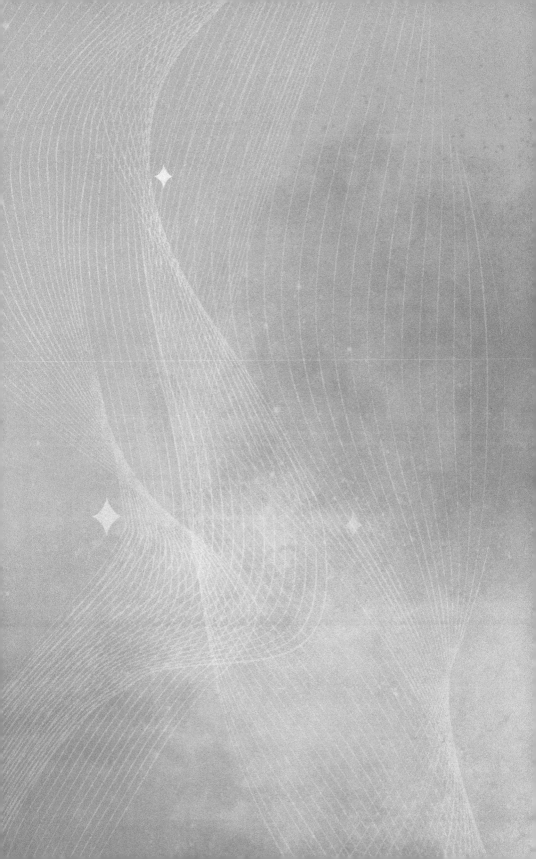

2

THROWING A SPELLBINDING COCKTAIL PARTY

Get ready to party as we fly you through
reasons to celebrate, with tips on buying
ingredients, spiritually setting up your
home, and making your party sparkle—plus
wrapping up your party and getting rid
of any nasty hangovers!

Hosting Your Coven

A coven is a group of witches who come together to perform spells and rituals. All are welcome! Having a hard time finding your coven? There are lots of ways to find your people! Explore online witchcraft/spiritual communities. (A note of caution: Do your research, so you know the community is a good fit for you.)

Utilize your talents, available ingredients, intuition, and—most important of all—love and light when making your chosen recipes. The key moral compass of Wicca is "harm none, do what you will." As such, there is no spell or incantation here meant to cause harm in any way.

A History of Gathering

Although it's not unlikely that a witch would practice on their own, there is a rich history of witches gathering to practice spells and rituals, most commonly around new and full moons. (And no, they're not usually naked.) The very reason the word "coven" was created is because witches often practice in groups. In Wicca, for example, after a year of studying, a new witch is initiated into the coven with a ceremony of celebration. Gathering with others is a witchcraft tradition that we encourage you to explore. There's power in numbers, baby!

How Much to Buy

Let's start planning our party! For a party of five people, we suggest at least two drink choices; for a party of 10, you'll want two or three drink choices; and for a party of 20, we advise five or six different cocktails.

So, what to serve? To select your recipes, first set the intention for your party. Is there a theme (new beginnings, full moon, a specific holiday)? Who's attending? Then, use this book to find the recipes that best suit your coven's needs. Remember, too, to choose recipes you feel comfortable making and are within your budget.

Keep in mind:

✦ 1 (750-ml) bottle = 16 cocktails

✦ 1 (1-L) bottle = 22 cocktails

- 1 (1.5-L) bottle = 33 cocktails
- 1 (750-ml) bottle of sparkling or still wine = 5 (5-ounce) servings
- Plus, plenty of ice!

Setting Up

You don't have to live in a penthouse with a view to throw an amazing party. What matters most is the vibe people feel. To create your magical vibe, focus on the senses: use scented candles or diffusers, string twinkle lights, or play fun music.

When accommodating a crowd, organization and preparation become your best friends. So, try these time-saving tips:

- Create simple syrups ahead of time.
- Make batch recipes in a serving pitcher (excluding carbonation, ice, and garnish), then refrigerate until needed. Just before serving, add the remaining ingredients, and shake or serve over ice as instructed.
- Prepare cocktail garnishes, then refrigerate on a plate covered with a damp cloth to keep them moist.
- Squeeze fresh fruit juice, and refrigerate in an airtight container.

Any space can serve as your bar as long as there's room for your ingredients and tools. If possible, locate the bar next to a sink and a trash can for convenience. Have plenty of towels handy for those accidental spills that inevitably occur!

Getting Your Home (Spiritually) Ready

Spiritually sprucing up your home is an essential step that can help you and your guests be comfortable. Here are our best tips:

BREAK OUT THOSE BROOMSTICKS: We know we said size doesn't matter, but cleanliness sure does! No one wants to be in your house if you haven't cleaned it in three weeks and they can smell your clumpy cat litter. Plus, cleaning and decluttering lifts dense and/or negative energy. Add a couple drops of essential oil (we recommend lemon for its cleansing properties) into your cleaning products. Add a spell: *I ask for assistance in cleaning and clearing this physical space. May I be guided through this process effortlessly.*

CLEANSE YOUR SPACE: When hosting your coven, energetic cleansing is just as important as physically cleaning. Sometimes referred to as smudging, energetic cleansing is the act of using plant material to remove negative energy and invite positive energy. The two most common tools for smudging are a sage bundle or a stick of palo santo. Open some windows so the smoke has somewhere to go. Light your chosen tool until it begins to smoke, then move around the space to fill it with smoke, holding an intention for cleansing, removing any unwanted energy, and inviting positive energy. But stay safe, buttercup! Hold a fire-safe receptacle to catch embers as you move around, and have a bowl of sand nearby to extinguish the burning matter once you finish the ritual.

KEEP YOUR FEET ON THE GROUND: In the mad dash and excitement of hosting a party, it's easy to feel flustered. When guests are arriving, you're getting texts because folks are lost or late, the dog is barking, you're being pulled in a thousand different directions, and you may be asking yourself, "Why did I throw this party in the first place?!" We totally get it. Hosting can have its stressful moments. To prevent feeling completely overwhelmed, center and ground yourself before guests arrive (see page 17). Take care of you, boo!

As two gals with healthy appetites—and an understanding that drinking alcohol on an empty stomach isn't good for anyone— we feel compelled to at least mention food!

A cocktail party is not meant to be dinner. That said, your gathering should have a variety of appetizers that people can nibble. Here are some suggestions to make sure nobody goes hungry, because that would be a damn shame.

Nutritious options (vegetarian and vegan friendly): bruschetta, fruit and/or veggie platter, hummus with pita, nuts

Savory: bacon-wrapped scallops, Buffalo chicken dip, caprese skewers (tomato, fresh basil, mozzarella), deviled eggs, meat and cheese board, meatballs, popcorn, prosciutto-wrapped asparagus or melon, spinach-artichoke dip

Sweets: chocolate-covered strawberries, cookies and brownies, s'mores (around a campfire if possible)

Reasons to Celebrate

Time to party! When you want to celebrate but don't have a birthday, holiday, or special event, celebrate a witchy holiday! Check out the Wheel of the Year, a nature-based calendar that represents eight different festivals/holidays important to many pagans, Wiccans, and witches. These festivals and holidays are not exclusive to those who practice witchcraft; anyone can participate in these magical celebrations. Here are our favorites!

WINTER SOLSTICE (YULE): DECEMBER 19–23

Celebrates the rebirth of the sun and the arrival of longer days. Traditional festivities include burning Yule logs and decorating trees, with the intention of protecting the home and bringing good luck.

SPRING EQUINOX (OSTARA): MARCH 19–23

Welcomes spring and the energy of fertility and an equal amount of daylight and dark hours. This is a time for planting seeds, both physical and metaphysical.

SUMMER SOLSTICE (LITHA): JUNE 19–23

The longest day of the year and a time to give thanks for a rich harvest (whatever that means for you). Often celebrated as a fire festival or solar festival, participants give thanks for agriculture and Earth's bounty.

AUTUMN EQUINOX (MABON): SEPTEMBER 20–24

Traditionally, a time when plants are harvested and autumn begins. A time to ground and find areas of balance in your life.

Helping All Feel Welcome

Got a party filled with introverts? Here are some tips to keep the party rolling.

WHAT'S YOUR NAME? Make proper introductions to those new to the group, highlighting something they might have in common with others.

MOCKTAILS ARE MAGIC. Have good options for people who don't drink alcohol, ideally, mocktail versions of the cocktails you're serving.

LET'S PLAY. A group activity or entertainment is always a fun way to keep people engaged. Hire a musician, or invite your talented friends to bring their instruments. See Getting Creative (page 31) for some fun ideas. Make participation optional—some people just prefer to watch.

MAKE IT A THEME. A costume or theme party is a fun way to get people talking! Add contests, if you like, and build your decorations and menu around the theme.

Getting Creative

Here are our favorite ways to incorporate magical elements into a party to make it even more mystical.

CANDLE MAGIC: Fill a large fireproof receptacle (such as a casserole dish) with sand, and set it on a sturdy surface where you can keep an eye on it during the party. Ask guests to decide on a goal they will hold in their mind during this ritual. Have available spell candles in different colors (a box of 40 online is less than $10). Explain what each candle color represents, and have guests select the appropriately colored candle based on their goal. Have each guest light their candle, stick it upright in the sand, and visualize their intention manifested. Let the candles burn throughout the party. Once the candles have burned out, give thanks for the positive energy coming your way.

HOROSCOPES: Before guests arrive, inquire about their birthdays, and research their horoscopes. Write them on cards, post in a place where everyone can read them, then vote on whom they think that horoscope represents. The person with the most correct answers wins a prize and some serious bragging rights.

MYSTERY CRYSTALS: Invite an expert to teach your coven about the magic of crystals. Have them bring samples to touch, hold, and feel so guests can get a sense of the crystal's energy. Explore how crystals can promote spiritual growth and healing and enhance rituals and spells. Or host a crystal swap, where each guest brings three crystals they're willing to swap.

TAROT READING: A tarot reader is a psychic who uses an ancient card deck, called tarot, to answer questions or offer counsel regarding specific circumstances, using their intuition and/or psychic ability to "read" the cards and interpret answers and possible future outcomes. Invite a tarot reader to talk about tarot and answer guests' questions, then have them do a collective reading for the group. You can also set up the reader in a separate room and offer individual mini sessions to your guests.

Wrapping Up

The party's over—you don't have to go home, but you can't stay here!

If you have a specific end time, a wonderful way to end your gathering is with a toast, thanking everyone for coming and highlighting some of the magical moments you shared. Express gratitude for your time together, and offer a parting spell for safe travels: *May you be protected as you travel and as you dream. I send you off with positive energy, as a part of my team.*

If your end time is open, take a few moments to thank each guest as they leave. After everyone has left, cleanse your space to clear any negative energy guests may have brought with them. This is a good practice any time you have company.

Hangover, Be Gone!

We hope you wake the next morning still riding high from your magical night! But in case you're feeling a little foggy, we've got some remedies.

H_2O TO THE RESCUE: Alcohol's most troublesome side effect (besides making you think it's a good idea to text your ex 17 times, enter a hot dog eating contest, or dance like no one is watching) is dehydration. Ideally, you'll incorporate water throughout your night of drinking; shoot for a ratio of one glass of water per cocktail. Then, before bed, drink at least one glass of water, and keep a full glass next to your bed so you can hydrate if you wake during the night. In the morning, start with a large glass of water, and hydrate throughout the day.

CHAMOMILE FOR HANGXIETY: What's hangxiety? It's that anxious feeling you sometimes wake up with after a night of drinking (if you don't know what we mean, good for you!). Chamomile tea is commonly used to calm overwhelming emotions, such as anxiety. It's also been known to relieve upset stomachs, which is also great for a hangover.

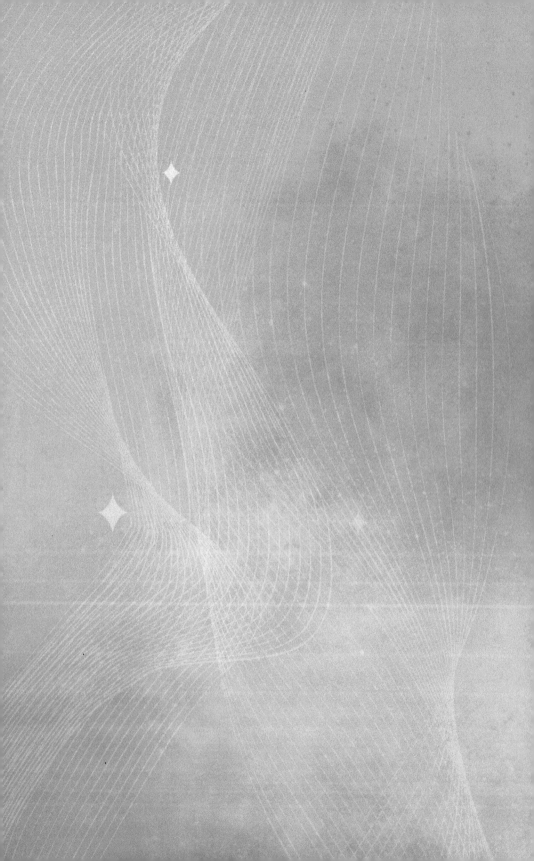

PART TWO

Spiritual LIBATIONS

It's time to get crafting! Here, you'll find recipes to ignite your imagination and conjure magic. Dive in, have fun, experiment, make mistakes, laugh, and—most important—drink and cast your spells responsibly!

3

LOVE & FRIENDSHIP

Mending Magic Potion   39

Divine Feminine   40

The Coven   41

Cupid's Cauldron   42

The Love Goddess   43

You've Got Mail   44

The Libido   45

The High Priestess Cosmo   46

A Witch's Best Friend   47

Pop My Cherry   48

The Good Witch   49

The Cauldron   50

The Seductress   51

SoulMate   52

Heart Chakra   53

Green Witch   54

All's fair in love and friendship! Who hasn't had to mend a broken heart, collect the pieces from a shattered friendship, or heal from a lack of self-love? We know we can't control other people or the karmic lessons the Universe gives us for personal growth. But we can put ourselves back in the driver's seat by working with energy and intention to manifest our reality. In this chapter, you'll learn how to brew magical potions to increase self-love, conjure up a soul mate, or even spice up the bedroom. So, dust off your cauldron, grab your wooden spoon, and get brewing!

Mending Magic Potion

Love and friendship aren't always warm and fuzzy. Sometimes, we suffer broken hearts, failed friendships, or the occasional knock-down, drag-out fight with a loved one. Rosemary and ginger have a magical ability to heal, and hibiscus is the ultimate supporter of love, whether that be with others or yourself. When mending a relationship, this potion is perfect to share.

TOOLS: citrus juicer, mug, cocktail shaker, tulip glasses

1 hibiscus tea bag
8 ounces hot water
2 ounces gin
1 ounce plus 2 teaspoons
  Cinnamon-Rosemary
  Simple Syrup (page 20)

Juice of ½ lemon
5 ounces ginger beer
2 rosemary sprigs

In a mug, combine the tea bag and hot water. Steep for 5 minutes. Remove and discard the tea bag; let the tea cool. Fill a cocktail shaker with ice. Pour in the gin, simple syrup, lemon juice, and tea. Cover and shake well. Pour the cocktail into two tulip glasses, top each with the ginger beer, and garnish each with a rosemary sprig.

SPELL / RITUAL: *While brewing this potion, be aware of what needs to be mended. Imagine a white, healing light engulfing you and/or your loved one. Allow this light to bring peace and resolution.*

Mocktail Magic: Omit the gin.

Divine Feminine

Embracing your divine feminine energy is more than just eating chocolate while PMSing, binge-watching Ryan Gosling movies, or spending an hour in the makeup aisle at CVS. Every person has divine feminine energy (including Ryan Gosling), which simply means that you're operating from an intuitive, receptive, heart-centered space. Tapping into your divine feminine energy allows your feelings to flow freely without judgment and with unconditional compassion and love.

TOOLS: cocktail shaker, strainer, chilled rocks glass

3 ounces whole milk
1½ ounces bourbon
½ ounce Cognac
1 ounce Vanilla Bean Simple Syrup (page 20)

½ teaspoon ground nutmeg
1 whole vanilla bean (optional)

Fill a cocktail shaker with ice, and pour in the milk, bourbon, Cognac, and simple syrup. Cover and shake until cold. Strain the drink into a chilled rocks glass. Garnish with the nutmeg and vanilla bean (if using).

SPELL / RITUAL: *Raise your glass, and repeat these words: I am a nonjudgmental and compassionate witness to all my feelings at this moment. So mote it be.*

Spellbinding Swap: Swap out the simple syrup for honey or agave nectar, and add a dash of vanilla extract.

The Coven

Heads up: This drink is meant to be shared! Please do not chug a scorpion bowl all by yourself like you're a freshman in college. The hangover won't be worth it . . . trust us. It features pineapple and orange, which are excellent at attracting good luck. Call your witchy pals together to make it a magical night of manifesting.

TOOLS: citrus juicer, scorpion bowl, bar spoon, long straws

2½ ounces gin
2½ ounces white rum
2½ ounces vodka
2½ ounces grenadine
1½ ounces dark rum

6 ounces pineapple juice
10½ ounces freshly
    squeezed orange juice
5 orange slices
6 Maraschino cherries

Fill a scorpion bowl or a large mixing bowl with ice. Add the gin, white rum, vodka, grenadine, dark rum, pineapple juice, and orange juice. Stir well. Garnish with the orange slices and cherries, and serve with long straws.

SPELL / RITUAL: *Sit in a circle with your coven, close your eyes, and hold hands while thinking about what you want to attract into your life. There's power in numbers! Let the collective energy amplify your wish.*

Batch Jt: Multiply the recipe by the number of scorpion bowls needed (we suggest two people per bowl).

Cupid's Cauldron

Let's cook up some romance! The tomato in this spicy little number is great for attracting or increasing passion, and the chili powder adds a magical kick to amplify this love spell. If you want Cupid's arrow to be on target, enjoy this drink while thinking of the one you desire.

TOOLS: citrus juicer, small dish, pint glass, cocktail shaker, bar spoon, strainer

1 teaspoon salt
1 teaspoon chili powder
2 lime wedges
6 ounces light Mexican beer (such as Corona)
3 ounces tomato juice

2 ounces freshly squeezed lime juice
2 teaspoons hot sauce (such as Frank's RedHot)
1 teaspoon Worcestershire sauce
1 teaspoon soy sauce

In a small shallow dish, stir together the salt and chili powder, and spread it to cover the bottom. Rub the rim of a pint glass with a lime wedge, then dip the rim into the chili salt to coat. Carefully fill the glass with ice. In a cocktail shaker, combine the beer, tomato juice, lime juice, hot sauce, Worcestershire sauce, and soy sauce. Stir well, then strain the drink into the prepared glass. Garnish with the remaining lime wedge.

SPELL / RITUAL: *Calling all singles! Standing in front of a mirror, repeat these words three times: If it's meant to be, may this person effortlessly come to me. So mote it be. Imagine any obstacles being resolved easily with love and light. Remember: We're not trying to get creepy here. Free will rules all.*

Mocktail Magic: Omit the beer.

The Love Goddess

Whether you're seeking new love, self-love, or rekindling an old flame, call upon Venus to assist with affairs of the heart. Venus is the Roman goddess of beauty, fertility, love, prosperity, and victory, and she is also the mother of Cupid, the god of love. Utilize the magical properties of cherries to attract and increase love in your life.

TOOLS: citrus juicer, cocktail shaker, bar spoon, strainer, flute glass

2 ounces cherry juice

2 ounces freshly squeezed orange juice

1 ounce bourbon

1 or 2 dashes Angostura bitters

3 Maraschino cherries

Fill a cocktail shaker with ice. Pour in the cherry juice, orange juice, and bourbon, then add the bitters. Stir to combine. Strain into a flute glass, and garnish with the cherries.

SPELL / RITUAL: *Raise your flute (pinky out, witch!), and repeat these words: Venus, help me open my heart, and guide me toward the light of love. Empower me to overcome any obstacles, negativity, and doubt that may be on my path to love. So mote it be.*

Spellbinding Swap: Use gin or vodka if you aren't a fan of bourbon.

You've Got Mail

We've all experienced being separated from people we love. Perhaps someone has moved, you're trying a long-distance relationship, or world affairs such as COVID-19 prevent you from seeing that special someone. Craft this concoction with ginger and orange peel, which can amplify your messages of love over space and time.

TOOLS: paring knife, citrus juicer, cocktail shaker, muddler, rocks glass, strainer

1 (½-inch) slice fresh ginger, peeled and coarsely chopped

1 (1-inch) piece orange peel

2 ounces brandy

1 ounce triple sec

1 ounce freshly squeezed lemon juice

2 teaspoons pure maple syrup

1 orange wheel

In a cocktail shaker, muddle the ginger and orange peel, then fill the shaker with ice. Pour in the brandy, triple sec, lemon juice, and maple syrup. Cover and shake vigorously. Place 1 large whiskey ice cube into a rocks glass, then strain the drink into it. Garnish with the orange wheel.

> SPELL / RITUAL: *Write a message of love on a piece of paper. Seal it in an envelope. Place a tealight candle on the envelope, and light the candle, letting it burn all the way down as the smoke carries your message of love to its intended recipient.*

Spellbinding Swap: Use whiskey or vodka instead of brandy.

The Libido

Get your juices flowing with this red-hot drink! Cayenne, known for sparking fiery passion when used in a love potion, can stir desire and ignite a thirst for life. Let this blazing hot cocktail fan the flames of even the most lukewarm love life! Feeling extra spicy? Add an extra pinch or two of cayenne.

TOOLS: small dish, muddler, cocktail shaker, strainer, rocks glass

1 (¾-inch-thick) fresh pineapple ring

2 ounces white rum

¾ ounce pasteurized egg whites

½ ounce Classic Simple Syrup (page 20)

⅛ teaspoon cayenne pepper

1 pineapple wedge

In a small dish, muddle the pineapple ring. Fill a cocktail shaker one-third full with ice, and strain the muddled pineapple juice into it. Pour in the rum, egg whites, and simple syrup, then add the cayenne. Cover and shake thoroughly to emulsify. Fill a rocks glass with ice, and strain the drink into it. Garnish with the pineapple wedge.

SPELL / RITUAL: *Add fire to your love life! Light two red candles, envision you and your lover, and repeat these words: With light and love, I invoke the power of fire with these flames. I now reignite our passion and love as we grow closer tonight. So mote it be. As the candles burn, move them closer together until they are right beside each other.*

Mocktail Magic: Replace the rum with lemonade.

The High Priestess Cosmo

Our take on the classic cosmopolitan! The High Priestess is a tarot card representing spiritual wisdom and intuition. Connect with this card to tap into your third eye (your energy center related to intuition and insight) to cultivate inner trust and follow that still, small voice inside that's got your back and knows you are a freakin' goddess.

TOOLS: citrus juicer, cocktail shaker, muddler, bar spoon, strainer, martini glass, cocktail spear

8 fresh cherries, pitted   **Juice of ½ lemon**
4½ ounces vodka   **1 ounce sparkling water**
1½ ounces triple sec   **1 lemon wheel**
¾ ounce grenadine

In a cocktail shaker, muddle 5 cherries. Add ice, and pour in the vodka, triple sec, grenadine, and lemon juice. Stir to combine. Strain into a martini glass, and top with the sparkling water. Drop a cherry into the bottom of the drink, then garnish with the lemon wheel and remaining 2 cherries, speared.

> SPELL / RITUAL: *Place one hand on your heart and the other on your third eye (at your forehead), connecting your heart to your intuition. Take three deep breaths, and imagine a cord of light connecting the two areas, allowing free-flowing energy and communication. Listen to what your inner voice has to say.*

Mocktail Magic: Omit the vodka, and add an equal amount of cranberry juice or ginger ale.

A Witch's Best Friend

Every witch needs their furry sidekick! Like witches, cats are creatures of the night, are fiercely independent, and seem to always have one foot in the spirit world. This potion will help you harness your inner cat to stay up all night and do what you want! May we suggest casting some epic spells under a full moon? It features coffee's magical properties, including revitalizing mental awareness and alertness.

TOOLS: cocktail shaker, strainer, martini glass

2 ounces vodka
2 ounces coffee liqueur
2 ounces espresso

½ ounce Vanilla Bean Simple Syrup (page 20)
1 teaspoon instant coffee

Fill a cocktail shaker with ice, and pour in the vodka, coffee liqueur, espresso, and simple syrup. Cover and shake vigorously. Strain into a martini glass. Garnish with the instant coffee.

SPELL / RITUAL: *Witches make their own rules, baby! Enjoy this magical cocktail anywhere you want, any time you want, any way you want.*

Mocktail Magic: Omit the coffee liqueur and vodka, and add more espresso.

Pop My Cherry

No, not *that* cherry ... just kidding—yes, that cherry! This potion features the potent properties of cherries, which are thought to increase fertility. And remember, you can give birth to more than just babies, people! With the right amount of effort, nurturing, and magic, anyone can birth an idea, a business, a garden, or a creative work of art. Let's plant that seed!

TOOLS: paring knife, cocktail shaker, muddler, bar spoon, rocks glass, strainer

3 Maraschino cherries
1 teaspoon cherry juice
3 ounces whiskey
¾ ounce Amaretto
½ ounce pure maple syrup

½ ounce Classic Simple
  Syrup (page 20)
3 dashes orange bitters
3 dashes Angostura bitters
1 orange peel

In a cocktail shaker, muddle the cherries with the cherry juice. Add an ice cube. Pour in the whiskey, Amaretto, maple syrup, and simple syrup. Add the orange bitters and Angostura bitters, and stir well. Place 1 ice cube into a rocks glass, then strain the drink into the glass. Garnish with the orange peel.

SPELL / RITUAL: *Ask yourself what you want to birth, then write it on a piece of paper. Bury the paper outside, in earth, as if planting a seed. Place your hand over the soil, and spend a few moments visualizing your wish being born.*

Spellbinding Swap: If you don't have Amaretto, use a dash of almond extract instead.

The Good Witch

Contrary to legends, myths, and popular belief, being a witch is about tapping into your spiritual abilities for the good of humanity and the planet. As we explain in our *Mystify Me* podcast, a witch is a natural healer who harnesses Universal energy and the gifts of Mother Earth. This potent cocktail will help you embrace your path as a healer and radiate light and love. Allow this libation to inspire psychic ability, healing, and most important: LOVE OF SELF.

TOOLS: citrus juicer, 2 small dishes, martini glass, cocktail shaker, bar spoon, strainer

½ ounce pure maple syrup
2 tablespoons sugar
8 ounces rosé wine
1½ ounces elderflower
  liqueur

Juice of ½ lemon
2 ounces sparkling water
Organic rose petals, for
  garnish

Pour the maple syrup into one small dish, and put the sugar into another. Dip the rim of a martini glass into the maple syrup, then into the sugar to coat the rim. Fill a cocktail shaker halfway with ice. Pour in the wine, liqueur, and lemon juice. Stir to combine. Strain the drink into the prepared martini glass, and top with the sparkling water. Float a rose petal or two on top.

SPELL / RITUAL: *Rose has the highest vibrational frequency of all flowers. Holding a long-stemmed rose (make sure it's pesticide-free), remove a petal, and drop it into the glass to infuse the cocktail with love and to honor the good witch within. As you take a sip, remove each petal from your rose, one by one, while identifying the qualities that make you divinely unique and magical. Raise your glass to your beautiful witchy self.*

The Cauldron

During the Middle Ages, women called brewsters could often be found at markets standing over large cauldrons brewing beer. Male brewers, in an attempt to dominate the beer industry, began a smear campaign accusing the brewsters of being witches. Many of the accused were forced to stop brewing—or even punished or killed. This cocktail honors and remembers all people who have been falsely accused and/or persecuted for being a witch.

TOOLS: citrus juicer, cocktail shaker, bar spoon, strainer, margarita glass

1½ ounces tequila
1½ ounces triple sec
Juice of ½ lemon
2 teaspoons honey

3 fresh mint leaves
6 ounces Mexican lager
1 mint sprig

In a cocktail shaker, stir together the tequila, triple sec, lemon juice, honey, and mint leaves. Add ice, cover, and shake. Pour in the beer, and strain the drink into a margarita glass. Garnish with the mint sprig.

SPELL / RITUAL: *Raise your glass to all your fallen homies. Repeat these words: I see you. I remember you. I honor you. May your soul be at rest. I carry your memory as an inspiration.*

Batch It: Get your coven together to honor your witchy ancestors. Multiply the recipe by the number of witches in your coven, combining all ingredients except the beer. Pour into a pitcher, and divide into margarita glasses. Top with beer, and raise one for your peeps!

The Seductress

Seduce yo' lover before someone else does! Fun fact: Throughout history, rosemary has been used in spells for fidelity and banishing jealousy. Married women would keep a bag of rosemary near their home's entrance because they believed it would ensure a faithful husband. In modern times, let's call upon rosemary's magical aphrodisiac qualities and whip up this intoxicating elixir. Have yourself a wild night, seductress!

TOOLS: citrus juicer, cocktail shaker, strainer, white wine glass

3 ounces whiskey

¾ ounce Amaretto

¾ ounce Cinnamon-Rosemary Simple Syrup (page 20)

Juice of ½ orange

3 dashes orange bitters

1 orange wheel

1 rosemary sprig

Fill a cocktail shaker with ice, and pour in the whiskey, Amaretto, simple syrup, and orange juice. Add the bitters. Cover and shake to combine. Strain the cocktail into a white wine glass. Garnish with the orange wheel and rosemary sprig.

SPELL / RITUAL: *Light a red candle, and let it burn, baby. Repeat these words three times: I am an irresistible, sexy, goddess/god. Then, seduce someone—or yourself.*

Spellbinding Swap: Swap out the Cinnamon-Rosemary Simple Syrup for Classic Simple Syrup (page 20), agave nectar, or honey.

Soul Mate

Okay, real talk: This cocktail is not going to manifest a soul mate for you (womp womp). As we discovered during our soul mates podcast episode, soul mates appear whenever they're good and ready. That said, it's possible to miss a soul mate if you don't have an open heart or have faulty preconceived notions of what they will look like. What this cocktail *can* do is help you clear any blockages you have, so you recognize your soul mate when the time is right.

TOOLS: citrus juicer, blender, cocktail shaker, strainer, martini glass

½ cup cubed watermelon
4 ounces tequila
3 ounces triple sec
1½ ounces freshly squeezed
　lime juice

2 teaspoons agave nectar
¾ ounce brandy
1 watermelon wedge

In a blender, blend the watermelon until pureed. Fill a cocktail shaker with ice, and add the watermelon puree, tequila, triple sec, lime juice, and agave. Cover and shake to chill, then strain the drink into a martini glass. Gently pour the brandy on top to float. Garnish with the watermelon wedge.

> SPELL / RITUAL: *First, remember that love magic has its limits, and what is meant to be will be. Get two similar-size seashells, soak them in water, pat them dry, and sprinkle dried rose leaves in them. Place a candle between the shells, light it, and repeat these words three times: I now open my heart to love and release all blocks to my soul mate. The cloud has lifted, and now I see. So mote it be.*

Mocktail Magic: Swap in lemonade or soda water for the tequila and triple sec.

Heart Chakra

The heart wants what it wants! The heart chakra is associated with unconditional love, compassion, forgiveness, and joy. This energy center affects every relationship we have, including the one with ourselves. Chocolate has long been used in cacao ceremonies to awaken, open, and heal the heart chakra. Call on chocolate's heart-expanding powers to attract a higher vibration of love, connection, and joy.

TOOLS: Irish coffee mug, bar spoon

**4 ounces hot chocolate
  (preferably dark)**
1½ ounces coffee brandy
**1½ ounces Irish cream
  liqueur**

1½ ounces vodka
Whipped cream, for topping
1 teaspoon cocoa powder

In an Irish coffee mug, combine the hot chocolate, coffee brandy, liqueur, and vodka. Stir. Top with whipped cream and the cocoa powder.

SPELL / RITUAL: *Lie down, and place a rose quartz crystal over your heart. Breathe deeply, and imagine a beautiful pink light coming from the crystal, filling your heart space. Visualize the pink light moving into every cell of your body, filling you with love and joy. Bask in the energy of love.*

Spellbinding Swap: For an extra kick, swap out the hot chocolate for freshly brewed coffee.

Green Witch

A green witch has the incredible ability to work with the power of Mother Nature and Universal energies for their spells and potions to create harmony and balance. Grapes are used to promote garden magic, while hibiscus amplifies love. Sip on this potent potion to honor Mother Earth and harness the power of the natural world around you.

TOOLS: Irish coffee mug, bar spoon, cocktail spear

4 ounces freshly brewed hibiscus tea
1½ ounces tequila
½ ounce green Chartreuse

1 ounce Vanilla Bean Simple Syrup (page 20)
1 mint sprig
3 green grapes

In an Irish coffee mug, stir together the hot tea, tequila, Chartreuse, and simple syrup. Garnish with the mint sprig and the grapes, speared.

SPELL / RITUAL: *Go outside, and sit with Mother Nature. Close your eyes, and tune in to your senses. Notice what you see, feel, hear, smell, and taste. Feel Mother Nature's energy pulsing through you.*

Spellbinding Swap: Swap out hibiscus tea for green tea.

4

BEGINNINGS & ENDINGS

Full Moon Magic 59

Mercury Retrograde 60

All Hallows' Eve 61

Witch's Wealth 62

The NDE 63

Eclipse 64

New Moon 65

The Phoenix 66

The Milky Way 67

Strawberry Moon 68

Summer Solstice 69

The Offering 70

Sea Witch 71

Waterworks Martini 72

Cosmic Sigh 73

When Life Gives You Lemons, Cast a Spell 74

Strap in, 'cause life's a bumpy road! The road is full of cycles and seasons, births and deaths, beginnings and endings. Change isn't always comfortable, but it's an essential part of growing, evolving, and becoming more of who you're meant to be. We truly believe that when one door shuts, another opens. Both experiences are an invaluable part of having a human experience, and both should be honored and celebrated. The potions, spells, and rituals in this chapter are designed to help you embrace beginnings and endings of all kinds, like marking a new opportunity, moving on from old patterns, or letting go of what no longer serves you.

Full Moon Magic

A witch's favorite night of the month! Full moon energy is a potent, powerful time of illumination. A time of letting go of the old and reaching for the new, the full moon offers a cleansing energy that helps us let go of emotions that need to be released. Take out your ice trays, fill them with water, cover with plastic wrap, and let them bask in the full moon's light to infuse the water with moon magic. Freeze and use the ice cubes to amplify the mystical powers of this cocktail.

TOOLS: vegetable peeler, highball glass, bar spoon

¾ ounce brandy
¾ ounce gin
¾ ounce dry vermouth

4 ounces ginger ale
1 lemon twist

Fill a highball glass with full moon ice. Pour in the brandy, gin, and vermouth. Stir gently, then add the ginger ale. Garnish with the lemon twist.

> SPELL / RITUAL: *Clean your crystals by placing them on a baking sheet and setting them outside or on a windowsill that gets moonlight. You can also make moon magic water by placing a sealed water-filled Mason jar under the full moon's light! Thank the moon for its magical cleansing help!*

Batch It: Multiply the ingredient amounts by the number of drinks needed. Combine all ingredients in a pitcher, except the ginger ale, then divide among the appropriate number of glasses. Top with the ginger ale, and garnish each with a lemon twist.

Mercury Retrograde

Relationship just ended? Have a crappy day at work? Blame it on Mercury retrograde . . . everyone else does! Mercury is known as the ruler of communication. Many people believe that Mercury retrograde is a time of miscommunication that, ultimately, can lead to failed relationships. Call upon pomegranate's magical ability to spark wisdom and instill patience during your communication with others.

TOOLS: food processor, fine-mesh sieve, medium bowl, bar spoon, margarita glass

7 fresh strawberries, hulled and halved, plus 1 slice	½ ounce grenadine
1 ounce vodka	5 ounces chilled dry prosecco
½ ounce elderflower liqueur	3 pomegranate seeds

In a food processor, puree the strawberry halves until smooth. Strain the strawberry puree through a fine-mesh sieve into a medium bowl. Stir in the vodka, liqueur, and grenadine, then pour the drink into a margarita glass. Tilt the glass slowly, and pour in the prosecco (this makes the drink foam). Gently stir, then garnish with the strawberry slice and pomegranate seeds.

SPELL / RITUAL: *Eat pomegranate seeds while sipping your cocktail. It is believed that the act of eating a pomegranate while holding a strong desire in your mind's eye is a powerful magical act and that your wish or desired wisdom will be granted.*

Spellbinding Swap: Instead of strawberries, try fresh raspberries. You can also use any sparkling wine you like.

All Hallows' Eve

Contrary to popular belief, Halloween isn't all candy corn and sexy cat costumes! Witches view Halloween as a time of transformation and change, as they give thanks for abundance and set intentions for the new year. It's also believed to be a time when the veil that separates the living from the dead is its thinnest, so it is a fabulous time to have a nice long chat with your spirit posse, ancestors, or friendly house ghost. This drink serves two for just that purpose.

TOOLS: vegetable peeler, saucepan, whisk, 2 Irish coffee mugs

8 ounces whole milk
½ cup sugar
¼ cup unsweetened cocoa powder
Pinch salt
1 cup canned pumpkin puree
1 teaspoon pumpkin pie spice

8 ounces vodka or vanilla vodka
8 ounces Kahlúa pumpkin liqueur
Whipped cream, for garnish
Shaved chocolate, for garnish

In a small saucepan, combine the milk, sugar, cocoa powder, and salt. Cook over medium heat, whisking, for 3 to 5 minutes, or until the sugar dissolves. Do not boil. Whisk in the pumpkin and pumpkin pie spice until fully combined. Remove from the heat, and immediately whisk in the vodka and Kahlúa. Divide between two Irish coffee mugs, and garnish each with whipped cream and chocolate.

> SPELL / RITUAL: *Halve an apple, and imagine filling the center of it with any bad habits, limiting beliefs, or negative energy, then put the halves back together. Bury the apple outside in the ground, letting go of what no longer serves you and planting seeds for the future.*

Witch's Wealth

Bring on the Benjamins! This is the perfect potion to conjure up during times of financial change or uncertainty. Call upon mint for its magical powers to promote prosperity and vitality or even to draw customers to your business.

TOOLS: cocktail shaker, bar spoon, strainer, rocks glass

2 ounces Cognac   **1 mint sprig**
1 ounce crème de menthe

Fill a cocktail shaker with ice, and pour in the Cognac and crème de menthe. Stir to chill. Strain the drink into a rocks glass, and garnish with the mint sprig.

SPELL / RITUAL: *Hold 3 mint sprigs, and use your senses to really experience them. What do they feel like, smell like, look like? Holding the mint in your hand, infuse it with your financial intentions. Tie the mint sprigs, and hang them upside down to dry. Place them wherever you make your living.*

Spellbinding Swap: No crème de menthe? Use peppermint schnapps.

 The NDE

Talk about death being the ultimate ending . . . or is it?! A near death experience (NDE) is an event in which someone dies for a short period of time and then comes back to life. Many report getting a glimpse into the spirit realm during this time, forever changing who they are and how they view the world. But you don't need such a dramatic event to positively shift your perspective on life. Draw on the cinnamon and rosemary in this potion to help you reflect and heal when needed.

TOOLS: paring knife, rocks glass, bar spoon

4 teaspoons Cinnamon-Rosemary Simple Syrup (page 20)
3 dashes orange bitters

2 ounces bourbon
1 strip orange peel
1 rosemary sprig
1 cinnamon stick

In a rocks glass, combine the simple syrup and bitters, then swirl to coat the inside of the glass. Fill the glass with ice, pour in the bourbon, add the orange peel, and stir. Garnish with the rosemary and cinnamon stick.

SPELL / RITUAL: *Light a green candle, which represents healing and growth. Call upon your spirit guides to send any messages of growth or insight you may need at this time.*

Spellbinding Swap: Swap out the bourbon for Irish whiskey.

Eclipse

Whether you're experiencing a lunar or solar eclipse, it's always a magical cosmic event. Eclipse energy helps you zoom in on areas in need of spiritual growth. These mystifying occurrences serve as catalysts for often abrupt beginnings and endings. It is a shocking yet necessary astrological push into the cold, deep end of the pool of change.

TOOLS: flute glass

4 ounces chilled Champagne   **3 ounces cola**
4 ounces chilled stout (such
  as Guinness)

Pour the Champagne into a flute glass. Slowly add the stout, then top with the cola.

SPELL / RITUAL: *Any ritual or spell done during this time will be amplified by powerful cosmic energy. Raise a glass, and repeat these words:* I welcome this powerful and benevolent eclipse energy of change. I trust it is always in my best interest and highest good. So mote it be.

Batch It: Multiply the recipe by the number of drinks needed.

New Moon

New moon, new you! The new moon signifies the beginning of a new lunar cycle. Its fresh energy marks new beginnings and a powerful time for course correction and manifesting. Pair this potion with the timing of a new project, goal, or habit to infuse your intentions with lunar magic.

TOOLS: vegetable peeler, flute glass

6 ounces Champagne or prosecco
2 dashes Angostura bitters

1 sugar cube
1 orange twist

Pour the Champagne into a flute glass, and add the bitters. Drop in the sugar cube, and garnish with the orange twist.

> SPELL / RITUAL: *Before you build your cocktail, determine what you'd like to call into your life in this next lunar cycle. As you drop the sugar cube into your glass, visualize this intention, and breathe it in.*

Batch It: Multiply the recipe by the number of drinks needed.

The Phoenix

Rise up, witches! The phoenix is a mythical bird representing resilience and resurrection. Connected to sun energy, the phoenix dies by bursting into flames but is reborn from its ashes, emerging stronger, wiser, and more powerful. You'll know when to brew this one.

TOOLS: citrus juicer, colada glass, bar spoon

1½ ounces tequila
6 ounces freshly squeezed orange juice
¾ ounce grenadine

1 ounce sparkling water
1 orange slice
1 Maraschino cherry

Fill a colada glass with ice, and pour in the tequila and orange juice. Slowly pour the grenadine into the glass over the back of a spoon, allowing it to settle at the bottom. Top with the sparkling water, and garnish with the orange slice and cherry.

SPELL / RITUAL: *If you have access to a fireplace or an outside firepit, light a fire. Identify an item (such as a receipt or a picture) that represents your past self. Throw the item into the fire with resolve, and watch it burn, transforming and rebirthing you.*

Spellbinding Swap: Exchange the tequila for vodka, or leave out the alcohol for a delicious mocktail.

The Milky Way

The Milky Way galaxy is home sweet home, and we live in the suburbs of this massive astrological body. Nothing gives you perspective like realizing that our sun is just one of more than 100 billion stars in this 13.51-billion-year-old cluster-f*ck of galactic goodness! Conjure up this marvelously milky concoction when you want to connect with something larger than yourself. Sit back, look up, and be in awe.

TOOLS: cocktail shaker, strainer, martini glass

1½ ounces whiskey
1½ ounces peanut butter whiskey
1½ ounces coffee liqueur

1½ ounces Irish cream liqueur
1½ ounces espresso
1 drop vanilla extract

Fill a cocktail shaker with ice, and pour in the whiskey, peanut butter whiskey, coffee liqueur, Irish cream liqueur, espresso, and vanilla. Cover and shake, then strain the drink into a martini glass.

SPELL / RITUAL: *On a clear night, take your concoction outside, and stargaze. Immerse yourself in the magic of the cosmos. Feel the connection, and draw on its power.*

Spellbinding Swap: If you don't have peanut butter whiskey, use more regular whiskey.

Strawberry Moon

The Strawberry Moon is, typically, the last full moon of June, heralding the transition from spring to summer. The name has been used by many Indigenous tribes to mark the ripening of the season's strawberry harvest and signal a time of great abundance. Strawberries are often used to celebrate a change of season, invoking happiness, harmony, and good luck.

TOOLS: blender, highball glass, fine-mesh sieve, bar spoon

4 fresh strawberries
2 fresh sage leaves
1½ ounces vodka

2 ounces sparkling water
¾ ounce crème de cassis

In a blender, combine 3 strawberries, the sage leaves, and vodka. Blend thoroughly. Fill a highball glass with ice, and using a fine-mesh sieve, strain the strawberry mixture into it. Add the sparkling water, and top with the crème de cassis. Stir, then garnish with the remaining strawberry.

SPELL / RITUAL: *Obviously, we recommend enjoying this libation under a Strawberry Moon, but any moon will do! Sit with your cocktail, and celebrate the change of season. Take a few deep breaths, reflect on where you've been, and ponder where you're going.*

Mocktail Magic: Substitute pink lemonade or cranberry juice for the vodka and crème de cassis.

Summer Solstice

Summer solstice marks the day of the year with the greatest number of daylight hours and the shortest night. It is spiritually significant in many faiths and often features bonfires to invoke fire magic, symbolizing the warmth and power of the sun. We love making this cocktail to help harness the power of nature to give momentum to new beginnings. This recipe features basil, which brings prosperity and opens the heart. Bottoms up, you sexy summer siren! PS: This recipe makes enough to share with a like-minded friend.

TOOLS: citrus juicer, small dish, 2 Collins glasses, cocktail shaker, muddler, strainer

1 tablespoon sugar
1 tablespoon ground cinnamon
6 fresh basil leaves, plus more for garnish
3 ounces white rum

2 ounces Strawberry Simple Syrup (page 20)
Juice of ½ lime
4 ounces sparkling water
1 fresh strawberry, sliced

In a small dish, combine the sugar and cinnamon. Wet the rims of two Collins glasses with water, then dip them into the cinnamon sugar to coat. In a cocktail shaker, muddle the basil leaves. Pour in the rum, simple syrup, and lime juice, then fill the shaker with ice. Cover and shake well. Carefully fill the two prepared glasses with ice, and strain the drink into them. Top with the sparkling water, and garnish with the strawberry slices and basil leaves.

SPELL / RITUAL: *Raise your glass, and repeat the following magical words: I invoke the power of fire and the sun to call in my most luminous and expanded self. As a divine, light-filled, powerful being, I now activate the power of the summer solstice to call [your intention, such as happiness, new career, love, financial abundance] into my life.*

The Offering

The universal Law of Reciprocity represents the idea of energy balance and mutual exchange. We see this all the time in nature; for example, when bees move from flower to flower collecting nectar, they also pollinate each flower. In the spirit of new beginnings, as opportunities or gifts come to you, consider giving an offering back to the Universe. This can be as simple as taking a moment to feel gratitude and give thanks for your good fortune.

TOOLS: citrus juicer, cocktail shaker, strainer, highball glass

1½ ounces white rum
¾ ounce crème de cassis
2½ ounces freshly squeezed orange juice

½ ounce cranberry juice
1½ ounces sparkling water
1 sage sprig

Fill a cocktail shaker with ice, then pour in the rum, crème de cassis, orange juice, and cranberry juice. Cover and shake well, then strain into a highball glass. Top with the sparkling water, and garnish with the sage.

SPELL / RITUAL: *Take in the aroma of the sage as you sip your cocktail. Close your eyes, and repeat these words as an offering of thanks: I am truly grateful for the gifts I have received. Allow your body, mind, and soul to fill with the warm, magical sensation of gratitude. Hold this feeling, and smile.*

Spellbinding Swap: Swap out the crème de cassis for Chambord, or increase the amount of cranberry juice.

Sea Witch

Sea witches have a powerful bond to the ocean and sea-faring life. They use elements of the seashore, such as coral, driftwood, sand, shells, and water, in their magic. The water element connects us to the ebb and flow of the human experience, encouraging us to embrace the fluidity and cycles of life. This gorgeous potion calls upon the wisdom of water magic, helping us honor and celebrate the tides of change.

TOOLS: vegetable peeler, cocktail shaker, strainer, martini glass

2 ounces gin
1 ounce blue curaçao
1 ounce peach schnapps

1 ounce sparkling water
(optional)
1 orange twist

Fill a cocktail shaker with ice, then pour in the gin, blue curaçao, and schnapps. Cover and shake until very cold. Strain into a martini glass. Top with the sparkling water (if using), and garnish with the orange twist.

SPELL / RITUAL: *Salt water is a powerful purifier, clearing your energy field and releasing negativity. Take a cleansing salt-water bath, ideally bathing in an ocean, or add Himalayan salt or Epsom salts to your bath.*

Spellbinding Swap: If you don't have a bathtub for this ritual, fill a bowl or bucket with warm salt water, and soak your feet.

Waterworks Martini

We're big believers in "it's better out than in." Ending a phase of life can bring up lots of emotion. This powerful potion will help you move that emotion so it doesn't become stuck or stagnant in the body. Watermelon's magical properties include aiding with emotional release and, most important, crying it out when you need to. So, grab a tissue, pour yourself a drink, and let it flow!

TOOLS: citrus juicer, blender, small dish, margarita glass, cocktail shaker, fine-mesh sieve, strainer, bar spoon

½ cup cubed watermelon
2 tablespoons sugar
2 ounces Strawberry Simple
    Syrup (page 20), plus more
    for the glass

4½ ounces vodka
¾ ounce dry vermouth
Juice of 1 lime
1 watermelon wedge
    or sage sprig

In a blender, blend the watermelon until pureed. Put the sugar in a small dish. Wet the rim of a margarita glass with simple syrup, then dip it into the sugar to coat. Fill a cocktail shaker with ice, and using a fine-mesh sieve, strain the puree into the shaker. Pour in the simple syrup, vodka, vermouth, and lime juice. Stir. Strain the drink into the prepared glass. Garnish with the watermelon wedge.

SPELL / RITUAL: *Set up a safe sacred space. Make it comfortable—lower the lights, wrap yourself in a blanket, and light a white candle to signify purification. Let all emotions move through you without any self-judgment. Once the candle burns out, light some sage, and smudge the room (and yourself), filling the room with smoke. Then, open the windows, and let the smoke carry the emotions away.*

Spellbinding Swap: No blender? Use a mortar and pestle or a fork to puree the watermelon.

Cosmic Sigh

Writer Ariana Palmieri calls the full moon a "cosmic sigh"—a time of the month when astrological energy peaks, then releases. This makes the full moon the perfect time to let go of negativity, to embrace forgiveness of yourself and others, and to prepare for new beginnings. This recipe features mint, a powerful healing herb that encourages the heart chakra to open, forgive, and let go.

TOOLS: citrus juicer, cocktail shaker, muddler, strainer, Cognac glass

¼ cucumber, peeled and sliced or coarsely chopped

12 fresh mint leaves, plus more for garnish

2 teaspoons agave nectar

2 ounces gin

Juice of 1 lime

1 cucumber wheel

In a cocktail shaker, muddle the cucumber, mint, and agave. Fill the shaker with ice, then pour in the gin and lime juice. Cover and shake vigorously until the cocktail is chilled to your liking. Strain the mixture into a Cognac glass. Garnish with mint leaves and the cucumber wheel.

SPELL / RITUAL: *On a piece of paper, write down what you are ready to release—spiritually and emotionally. Hold your paper, and repeat the following magical words three times: I now release you. I now release you. Thank you for the lessons you have taught me. It is time for you to move on, so mote it be. If you so choose, throw the paper in the trash, or safely burn it.*

Spellbinding Swap: Swap out the agave for Classic Simple Syrup (page 20).

When Life Gives You Lemons, Cast a Spell

Okay, look, sometimes life really kicks you where the sun don't shine. But we're here to help! We believe that endings are bittersweet and offer opportunities for spiritual growth amid the heartache. A failed relationship, being let go from a job, or the death of a loved one are all tragically painful. They are also catalysts for change—and it's up to you whether to harness and direct that energy toward creating the life you want. In this recipe, we call upon lemon's magical cleansing properties to release and remove any negative residue from a difficult situation so you can walk toward a bright future!

TOOLS: citrus juicer, 2 small dishes, martini glass, cocktail shaker, strainer, zester

1 teaspoon honey
1 teaspoon sugar
2 ounces vodka

4 ounces lemonade
Juice of 1 lemon (save the lemon for zesting)

Pour the honey onto a small dish. Place the sugar in another small dish. Dip a martini glass into the honey, then into the sugar to coat. Fill a cocktail shaker with ice, and pour in the vodka, lemonade, and lemon juice. Cover and shake vigorously. Strain the drink into the prepared glass. Garnish by zesting the reserved lemon on top.

SPELL / RITUAL: *Fill the bathtub with warm water, squeeze in fresh lemon juice, lemon slices, and/or add lemon essential oil. As you soak in the tub, imagine any negative energy or emotions seeping out into the bathwater, washing away any residue that may be holding you back.*

Mocktail Magic: Omit the vodka, and substitute with soda water or more lemonade.

5

HEALTH & HEALING

The Magic Wand	79
Light & Love	80
Stardust	81
Empath Elixir	82
Wicked Sexy Witch	83
Lavender Elixir	84
Sleeping Beauty	85
Bewitching Beauty	86
Milk Magic	87
Blood Moon	88
Berry Brew	89
The Healer	90
The Amethyst	91
Fountain of Youth	92
✦ Cucumber Charm	93
Cosmic Cleanse	94

Keep your wicked witch at bay by staying healthy and happy! These recipes are designed to promote health and healing on all levels—emotional, mental, physical, and spiritual. Read on to see how the magical powers of herbs and intentions can help rid flu symptoms, calm anxiety, enhance sleep, and even relieve PMS pains. You'll be brewing healing potions before you know it!

The Magic Wand

This earthy tequila martini is filled with magical healing powers and health benefits. Olives carry loads of anti-oxidants and tons of vitamin E while also supporting heart function and protecting against osteoporosis and cancer. Thyme, rosemary, and basil are all great sources of vitamin A, magnesium, and iron. Bottoms up, witches!

TOOLS: small bowl, muddler, small dish, chilled martini glass, cocktail shaker, bar spoon, strainer, cocktail spear

½ teaspoon fresh rosemary leaves

½ teaspoon fresh thyme leaves

½ teaspoon chopped fresh basil leaves

¾ ounce olive brine

1 teaspoon salt

3 ounces tequila

2 green martini olives

In a small bowl, muddle the rosemary, thyme, basil, and olive brine. Let sit for 30 minutes. Pour the salt into a small dish. Wet the rim of a chilled martini glass with water, then dip it into the salt to coat. Fill a cocktail shaker with ice, add the herb mixture, and pour in the tequila. Gently stir, then strain the drink into the prepared glass, and garnish with the olives, speared.

SPELL / RITUAL: *Grab your magic wand (a stick from the garden, a sage stick, a selenite stick, even a wooden spoon will do)! Wave your wand around your body, repeating these words three times and slowly spinning clockwise: Cold, flu, and germs be gone. Healthy body from now on. So mote it be.*

Spellbinding Swap: Swap out the tequila for vodka or even gin.

Light & Love

Raise that vibration by calling in the energy of light and love! Strawberries are thought to hold one of the highest vibrational frequencies of any food and are associated with light, growth, and abundance. And they do a body good! These gorgeous little berries are full of nutrients, including fiber, manganese, and potassium, and they boast particularly high levels of antioxidants. Use this recipe when you need to ignite a fire of love and light within and keep a healthy body, mind, and soul.

TOOLS: citrus juicer, cocktail shaker, bar spoon, margarita glass

6 ounces light beer
1½ ounces tequila
8 ounces pink lemonade
Juice of ½ lemon

¾ ounce Strawberry Simple Syrup (page 20)
1 lemon wheel
1 fresh strawberry

In a cocktail shaker, combine the beer, tequila, lemonade, lemon juice, and simple syrup. Stir gently. Fill a margarita glass with ice, and pour the cocktail into it. Garnish with the lemon wheel and strawberry.

SPELL / RITUAL: *Inscribe your name on a white candle, signifying purification, and light it while repeating these words three times: This fire's light burns my ailments away. Health and wellness are here to stay. When the candle has burned out, say: So mote it be.*

Spellbinding Swap: Use Classic Simple Syrup (page 20) instead of strawberry.

Stardust

When you wish upon a star . . . you feel a hell of a lot better! Vanilla beans have purifying, restorative energy, much like the light of a star. Vanilla also increases positive energy and strengthens mental abilities. Vanilla pairs perfectly with chamomile in this healing and transformative concoction. Prepare this potion to help you harness the power of a wish for a health or healing goal.

TOOLS: mug, fine-mesh sieve, cocktail shaker, wine glass

½ cup dried chamomile flowers
8 ounces hot water

1½ ounces Vanilla Bean Simple Syrup (page 20)
3 ounces tequila
1 vanilla bean (optional)

Put the chamomile in a large mug, and pour the hot water over it. Steep for 5 to 10 minutes, then let cool. Using a fine-mesh sieve, strain the tea into a cocktail shaker. Add the simple syrup and tequila, then cover and shake. Fill a wine glass (red or white) with ice, and pour the drink over it. Garnish with the vanilla bean (if using).

SPELL / RITUAL: *Wrap yourself in a comfy blanket, go outside, and stargaze. Make a wish upon a star, and allow the light of that star to cast its calming energy on you. Repeat these words: This magical star grants thee, with good intention and purity. So mote it be.*

Spellbinding Swap: Swap in rum for the tequila.

Empath Elixir

As self-diagnosed empaths, we are constantly exploring ways to navigate the energy-filled world around us.
Being sensitive to energy can sometimes leave you feeling
depleted and anxious. As we discovered while researching
for our podcast episode about empaths, lavender is superb
for relieving anxiety and promoting a calm, clear mind
and spirit.

TOOLS: mug, cocktail shaker, fine-mesh sieve, strainer,
martini glass

**1½ tablespoons dried
  culinary-grade lavender**
4 ounces hot water
**¾ ounce Mint Simple Syrup
  (page 20)**

2 ounces grape juice
2 ounces sparkling wine
1 mint sprig

Put the lavender in a large mug, and pour the hot water over
it. Steep for 5 to 10 minutes, then let cool. Fill a cocktail shaker
with ice. Using a fine-mesh sieve, strain the lavender tea into
the shaker, and pour in the simple syrup and grape juice. Cover
and shake. Strain the drink into a martini glass, and top with the
sparkling wine. Garnish with the mint sprig.

SPELL / RITUAL: *Burn incense (we recommend frankincense),
and repeat these words three times: Cloudy thoughts flee
quickly. Let lavender strengthen clarity. Strength of mind, come to
me. So mote it be.*

Mocktail Magic: Swap out the sparkling wine for sparkling water.

Wicked Sexy Witch

Bow-chicka-bow-wow *wow*—it's time to liven up that libido, you sexy witch! Blackberries are loaded with vitamins C and E as well as phytochemicals, which boost sexual performance and drive. So, slip into something comfortable, spin up this sassy little libation, and get ready for a satisfying evening with that special someone . . . or fly solo, you sexy beast.

TOOLS: citrus juicer, cocktail shaker, bar spoon, pint glass

1½ ounces whiskey
¾ ounce Blackberry Simple Syrup (page 20)
¾ ounce freshly squeezed lime juice

¾ ounce grenadine
8 ounces Irish stout
2 fresh blackberries

In a cocktail shaker, stir together the whiskey, simple syrup, lime juice, and grenadine. Pour in the stout, add ice, and stir again to mix. Pour the drink into a pint glass. Float the blackberries on top.

> SPELL / RITUAL: *Inscribe a red candle with your name and your lover's name. Light the candle as you repeat these words: Allow love and passion to flow freely between our souls tonight, igniting our love as we join together through light. So mote it be. Place rose petals on and under your bed to amplify the vibration of your bedroom.*

Spellbinding Swap: With their high amount of vitamin B (which supports a healthy sex life), blueberries are a great swap for blackberries.

Lavender Elixir

Lavender is known to lift spirits, ease anxiety, and enhance relaxation. It can also help reduce pain and inflammation and speed up the healing process by increasing circulation. Infusing your space with lavender can help you call in a peaceful, grounded energy whenever you need to soothe your soul. We love to sip this sweet, refreshing drink while sitting outside breathing in fresh air and soaking up the sun.

TOOLS: citrus juicer, mortar and pestle, 2 small dishes, Collins glass, cocktail shaker, strainer

1 tablespoon dried culinary-grade lavender
1 tablespoon sugar
1 teaspoon honey
1½ ounces sweet tea vodka
1½ ounces bourbon

¾ ounce triple sec
¾ ounce Honey-Lavender Simple Syrup (page 20)
Juice of 1 lemon
2 dashes lavender bitters
1 organic lavender sprig

In a mortar and using a pestle, grind together the lavender and sugar to release the lavender oils. Transfer the lavender sugar to a small dish. Drizzle the honey over another small dish. Chill a Collins glass with ice, then dip the rim into the honey and into the lavender sugar to coat. Fill a cocktail shaker with ice, and pour in the vodka, bourbon, triple sec, simple syrup, and lemon juice. Add the bitters. Cover and shake well. Strain the drink into the prepared glass. Garnish with the lavender sprig.

SPELL / RITUAL: *Sip this elixir, and repeat these words three times: Surround me in positive ways, encompass me, and mend my being. Shower me with radiant light so I stay healthy and well in the coming days. So mote it be.*

Spellbinding Swap: Use regular vodka or another sweet-flavored vodka you like instead of the sweet tea vodka.

Sleeping Beauty

Wake up feeling as rested as Sleeping Beauty! Lavender is renowned for its ability to induce relaxation, making it the perfect spiritual tool to help ease and clear the mind for a restful night's sleep. Chamomile is a powerful complement to this potion, as its magical energy soothes anxiety, reduces stress, and supports deep, restorative sleep.

TOOLS: saucepan, fine-mesh sieve, Irish coffee mug

8 ounces water
2 tablespoons dried culinary-grade lavender
2 tablespoons dried whole chamomile flowers

2 tablespoons dried lemon balm leaf
1 tablespoon sugar
2 ounces brandy

In a small saucepan, combine the water, lavender, chamomile, lemon balm, and sugar. Bring to a boil over high heat. Reduce the heat to low. Simmer for 5 to 10 minutes. Remove from the heat. Using a fine-mesh sieve, strain the mixture into an Irish coffee mug. Discard the solids. Add the brandy to float on top.

> SPELL / RITUAL: *Place the lavender, chamomile, and lemon balm in a small drawstring bag. Close and tie the bag as you repeat these words three times:* I now release any thoughts and energy that no longer serve me. I allow calming and relaxing energy to flow through me freely. Flowing and drifting, drifting and flowing, flowing and drifting. Effortlessly and peacefully falling into sleep tonight. So mote it be. *Place the sleep spell bag under your pillow or bed.*

Mocktail Magic: Omit the brandy.

Bewitching Beauty

Be your beautiful self with this bountiful potion. Known for its powerful cleansing properties, lemon is commonly used in spells for purification, detoxification, and space clearing. Lemon offers amazing benefits to the body by strengthening the immune system, balancing pH levels, and assisting with digestion. With its natural antibacterial properties, lemon also promotes the production of healthy enzymes, which help the liver flush toxins from the body.

TOOLS: citrus juicer, cocktail shaker, strainer, flute glass

1½ ounces gin
¾ ounce cranberry juice
¾ ounce Classic Simple Syrup (page 20)

Juice of ½ lemon
3 ounces sparkling wine
1 lemon wheel

Fill a cocktail shaker with ice, and pour in the gin, cranberry juice, simple syrup, and lemon juice. Cover and shake, then strain the drink into a flute glass. Top with the sparkling wine, and garnish with the lemon wheel.

SPELL / RITUAL: *In a small bowl, combine 6 tablespoons salt and several lemon slices. Place this bowl beside or under your bed. The lemon and salt will cleanse your space, repelling any negative energies, to ensure a peaceful and protected night's sleep. Ensure you place this spell safely out of reach from pets.*

Spellbinding Swap: Use any kind of sparkling wine you have on hand, like Champagne or prosecco. You can also add sparkling water to white wine to create the same effect.

Milk Magic

Let's milk this one for all it's worth! Once a common offering to the gods, milk is strongly tied to spiritual growth and connection. With its nourishing energy and ability to manifest beauty, milk is the magic in this sweetly scrumptious cocktail.

TOOLS: cocktail shaker, red wine glass

3 ounces coffee brandy

3 ounces vodka

3 ounces 1% milk

¾ ounce half-and-half

¾ ounce Vanilla Bean Simple Syrup (page 20)

½ teaspoon ground cinnamon

½ teaspoon ground nutmeg

3 coffee beans

1 cinnamon stick

Fill a cocktail shaker with ice, and pour in the brandy, vodka, milk, half-and-half, and simple syrup. Cover and shake, then pour the drink into a red wine glass. Sprinkle on the cinnamon and nutmeg. Float the coffee beans on top, and garnish with the cinnamon stick.

SPELL / RITUAL: *Draw yourself a nourishing milk bath by adding 1 to 2 cups powdered milk to a warm bath. A milk bath can be soothing and healing for conditions such as dry skin, eczema, poison ivy, psoriasis, sunburn, or a really bad day.*

Spellbinding Swap: Don't have coffee brandy? Brew some espresso or coffee for a replacement.

Blood Moon

Mama said there'd be days like this! But ladies, we've found a silver lining to riding that crimson wave every month: it's a great excuse to craft this cleansing concoction! The Blood Moon, a lunar event that happens when the moon is in total eclipse, is said to bring in new beginnings and clear blockages that no longer serve your highest good. Whip up this potion when you need some extra support during that time of the month, and take care of yourself, gorgeous!

TOOLS: pint glass, bar spoon, cocktail spear

- 2 ounces vodka
- 3 ounces tomato juice
- 1 teaspoon olive brine
- 5 dashes Worcestershire sauce
- 3 dashes Tabasco
- 1 teaspoon prepared spicy horseradish
- ¼ teaspoon freshly ground black pepper
- ⅛ teaspoon garlic powder
- 3 olives

Fill a pint glass three-quarters full with ice. Pour in the vodka, tomato juice, and olive brine, then add the Worcestershire sauce, Tabasco, horseradish, pepper, and garlic powder. Stir well. Garnish with the olives, speared.

SPELL / RITUAL: *Cinnamon, clove, lavender, and rose essential oils (make sure you're not allergic) are all thought to alleviate menstrual cramps. Combine a few drops with a carrier oil, such as coconut or extra-virgin olive oil, and massage into your abdomen while repeating these words: Clear my uterus, release my pain, so I can be healthy once again. So mote it be.*

Mocktail Magic: Replace the vodka with more tomato juice.

Berry Brew

We love this recipe so berry much! Berries are renowned as one of the healthiest foods on Earth, and for good reason. They're loaded with antioxidants, packed with nutrients, and have potent anti-inflammatory properties. Not to mention, they support wound healing and skin regeneration while reducing toxic free radicals in the body. Talk about packing a punch! Enjoy this berry-licious beverage—bottoms up!

TOOLS: cocktail shaker, muddler, strainer, flute glass

14 fresh blueberries
9 fresh blackberries
3 ounces whiskey

½ ounce Blackberry Simple Syrup (page 20)
Dry Champagne, chilled, for topping

In a cocktail shaker, muddle the blueberries and 6 blackberries. Pour in the whiskey and simple syrup. Add ice, cover, and shake vigorously. Strain the drink into a flute glass, and top with Champagne. Garnish with the remaining 3 blackberries.

SPELL / RITUAL: *Fill a bowl with berries, ice water, and three floating candles. As you light the candles, repeat these magical words: Protect me from illness all around, a magical shield from my head to ground. This virus will not pass through me, for I am strength. So mote it be. Once the candles have burned out, eat the berries to summon health and wellness.*

Mocktail Magic: Get all of the berry magic without the booze! Replace the whiskey with lemonade or cranberry juice.

The Healer

Sage takes the stage in this magical healing potion. Widely recognized by witches everywhere for cleansing the mind, body, and spirit, sage is the optimal healing herb. Call upon the fresh sage leaves in this luscious libation for their anti-inflammatory powers and to promote longevity.

TOOLS: cocktail shaker, muddler, bar spoon, snifter glass, strainer

1½ ounces Cognac Brandy
2 fresh sage leaves

½ ounce crème de menthe
2 ounces sparkling water

In a cocktail shaker, muddle the Cognac and sage leaves, leaving the sage mostly intact. Pour in the crème de menthe, and add ice. Stir to chill. Fill a snifter glass with ice, and strain the drink into it. Top with the sparkling water.

SPELL / RITUAL: *Fill a small bowl or reusable tea bag with salt, and hold the bowl in front of your mouth. Exhale fully into the salt three times, imagining the illness in your body as a smoke or steam leaving your body. Imagine the salt absorbing and drawing out the illness. Flush the salt down the toilet as you repeat these words: Cold, flu, and ills be gone. Healthy body from now on. So mote it be.*

The Amethyst

Lavender again for the win! Much like the beautiful amethyst crystal, lavender is known for its magical healing properties for both body and mind. It encourages relaxation, soothes anxiety, and reduces mind chatter. Feeling like your nerves are frayed? Whip up this recipe, take a deep breath, and allow lavender's gentle spirit to soothe your soul.

TOOLS: citrus juicer, mortar and pestle, small dish, Collins glass, cocktail shaker, muddler, strainer

1 tablespoon dried
   culinary-grade lavender
1 tablespoon sugar
1 lemon slice
12 fresh mint leaves
1½ ounces Classic Simple
   Syrup (page 20)

4 ounces gin
1½ ounces peach schnapps
Juice of ½ lemon
4 dashes lavender bitters
1 stick purple rock candy

In a mortar and using a pestle, grind together the lavender and sugar to release the lavender oils, then transfer to a small dish. Chill a Collins glass with ice, and wet the rim of the glass with the lemon slice. Dip the rim into the lavender sugar to coat, and carefully fill the glass with ice. In a cocktail shaker, muddle the mint and simple syrup, then pour in the gin, schnapps, and lemon juice. Add the bitters. Cover and shake, then strain the drink into the prepared Collins glass. Garnish with the rock candy.

SPELL / RITUAL: *Hold fresh lavender in your right hand and an amethyst in your left hand. Close your eyes, and repeat these words as many times as needed to allow a feeling of peace to wash over you: This magical crystal anoints thee. With all things good, magically. So mote it be.*

Spellbinding Swap: Replace the gin with vodka.

Fountain of Youth

Eternal youth? Yes, please! Okay, this potion won't give you eternal youth, but it will help you tap into the magical powers of lemon, largely considered the master purifier of the witch-craft world! It is the go-to for clearing the mind, body, and spirit. Lemon is also associated with the moon and water elements, making it a powerful tool for full-moon spellcasting. Tap into lemon's energy and cleansing properties to clear spaces and items and promote positivity within relationships.

TOOLS: citrus juicer, cocktail shaker, Collins glass, strainer

3 ounces vodka
1½ ounces sweet tea vodka
Juice of 1 lime
Juice of ½ lemon
1½ ounces Classic Simple
   Syrup (page 20)

2 dashes orange bitters
4 or 5 fresh mint leaves,
   chopped
1 lemon wedge
1 mint sprig

Fill a cocktail shaker with ice, and pour in the vodka, sweet tea vodka, lime juice, lemon juice, and simple syrup. Add the bitters and mint leaves. Cover and shake vigorously. Fill a Collins glass with ice, and strain the drink into it. Garnish with the lemon wedge and mint sprig.

SPELL/RITUAL: *We believe that self-love is the magic secret to the fountain of youth! Slice a lemon, and place the pieces in a bath or your shower. As you do this cleansing ritual, repeat these words: Water, water, wash away. Water, water, clearance today. Love within, love without. I love myself without doubt. So mote it be.*

Batch It: Multiply the recipe by the number of drinks needed. Pour the first seven ingredients into a large ice-filled pitcher, then strain into Collins glasses. Garnish with lemon wedges and mint sprigs.

Cucumber Charm

Who knew cucumber was such a VIP in the vegetable world?! This hydrating plant has tons of healing properties and, for years, has been used to treat exhaustion, hangovers, swelling, and more! Cucumber also helps balance our feminine and masculine energies.

TOOLS: cocktail shaker, muddler, bar spoon, rocks glass

1 (½-inch) piece cucumber, peeled and coarsely chopped
¾ ounce Aperol
1½ ounces vodka
¾ ounce lemonade
3 ounces sparkling water
1 cucumber slice

In a cocktail shaker, thoroughly muddle the cucumber and Aperol. Fill the shaker with ice, and pour in the vodka, lemonade, and sparkling water. Stir, then pour the drink into a rocks glass. Garnish with the cucumber slice.

SPELL / RITUAL: *Inscribe your name and the words "good health" on a yellow candle. Safely light the candle, lie down, and place cucumber slices on your eyes while visualizing your body as healthy and whole. Once the candle has completely burned out, repeat these words: So mote it be.*

Mocktail Magic: Replace the Aperol and vodka with cranberry juice and/or sparkling water.

Cosmic Cleanse

Cleanse baby, cleanse! We all need a good clearing out now and again! This potion calls upon lime and grapefruit for their incredible magical healing and cleansing properties. Both fruits are high in antioxidants and are known in the witchcraft world for their purification abilities.

TOOLS: citrus juicer, cocktail shaker, strainer, coupe glass

3 ounces white rum
Juice of ½ lime
Juice of ½ grapefruit
½ ounce grenadine

½ ounce Classic Simple Syrup (page 20)
1 lime wedge

Fill a cocktail shaker with ice. Pour in the rum, lime juice, grapefruit juice, grenadine, and simple syrup, then cover and shake well. Strain the drink into a coupe glass, and garnish with the lime wedge.

SPELL / RITUAL: *Rub a grapefruit wedge along your neck, arms, and hands, allowing it to cleanse you. Breathe in the bright aroma, and repeat these words three times: My body, mind, and spirit are now purified, cleansed, and fully restored. So mote it be.*

Batch It: Multiply the recipe by the number of drinks needed. Pour the first five ingredients into a large ice-filled pitcher, then stir and strain into coupe glasses. Garnish with lime wedges.

6

CELEBRATIONS &
SPIRITUAL GROWTH

Autumn Equinox   99

Sun Sacrifice   100

Hedge Witch   101

Crystal Ball   102

Samhain Spirits   103

The Brewster   104

Selene's Secret   105

Midnight Magic   106

Sixth Sense   107

Mother Earth   108

Mystify Me   109

The Athena   110

The Mermaid   111

The Money Maker   112

The Spicy Ginger   113

Karmic Boost   114

t's time to cultivate your magnificent inner witch! This chapter is designed to help you embrace your spiritual side while offering amazing excuses to celebrate, no matter the time of year. We'll cover everything from expanding your intuition to honoring abundance and connecting with your spirit posse. Whether you choose to enjoy these cocktails alone or with your coven, remember, there's always something to celebrate!

Autumn Equinox

The autumn equinox represents the harvest of the season's abundance. The cranberries in this recipe symbolize abundance and gratitude, reminding us to celebrate all the wonderful things we have cultivated throughout the year. What better way to give thanks than with a beautifully witchy cocktail in hand?

TOOLS: citrus juicer, cocktail shaker, strainer, coupe glass

1½ ounces gin
Juice of ½ lemon
1 ounce cranberry juice

½ ounce pure maple syrup
3 ounces sparkling wine
3 fresh cranberries

Fill a cocktail shaker with ice, and pour in the gin, lemon juice, cranberry juice, and maple syrup. Cover and shake until cold. Strain the drink into a coupe glass, and top with the sparkling wine. Garnish with the cranberries.

SPELL / RITUAL: *Prepare a meal that represents autumn, including a bounty of beautiful foods such as fresh fruits, vegetables, and nuts. As you enjoy the meal, reflect upon and give thanks for what you have manifested since summer solstice.*

Mocktail Magic: Omit the gin, and use a nonalcoholic sparkling wine.

Sun Sacrifice

Who couldn't use a little more sunshine in their life? The sun is a powerful symbol of energy, positivity, clarity, and confidence. Pineapples are connected to the sun's ability to call in growth and enlightenment. Tap into the transformative element of the sun with this bright and beautiful cocktail, and bask in the sun's spectacular magic!

TOOLS: cocktail shaker, muddler, tulip glass, strainer, cocktail spear

1 pineapple ring
¾ ounce Vanilla Bean Simple Syrup (page 20)
3 ounces white rum

¾ ounce triple sec
Pineapple chunks, for garnish

In a cocktail shaker, muddle the pineapple ring and simple syrup. Pour in the rum and triple sec. Cover and shake vigorously to froth. Fill a tulip glass with ice, and strain the drink into it. Garnish with 3 or 4 pineapple pieces, speared.

SPELL / RITUAL: *Find a sunny spot. Imagine a ball of golden light entering the top of your head, and feel the energy of the sun entering your body. Focus on the sun warming your hair and radiating down your body, traveling along your spine and all the way out of your arms and legs. Envision yourself glowing with powerful golden light from the inside out.*

Mocktail Magic: Replace the rum with pineapple juice.

Hedge Witch

No gardening tools needed! Hedge witches are known for practicing hedge jumping, which is crossing the boundary between this world and the spirit world. In addition to psychic communication and astral projection, these witches are also skilled in herbal arts and magic involving Earth elements. Allow the magic of elderflower to help you connect to the spirit realm, and open your psyche to see things in a new, positive light.

TOOLS: citrus juicer, cocktail shaker, bar spoon, chilled rocks glass

3 ounces gin
1 ounce elderflower liqueur
1½ ounces freshly squeezed grapefruit juice

3 ounces tonic water
1 rosemary sprig

Fill a cocktail shaker with ice. Pour in the gin, liqueur, and grapefruit juice. Stir, and pour into a chilled rocks glass. Top with the tonic water, and garnish with the rosemary sprig.

SPELL / RITUAL: *Sit outside, or open windows and doors, allowing the wind to flow freely. Repeat these words: Open my eyes, open my mind, please allow the messages to arrive. If voices are near, please open my ears, and allow me to hear.*

Spellbinding Swap: Not into gin? Swap it out for vodka!

Crystal Ball

We see a deliciously delightful drink in your future! In ancient cultures, witches would stare deeply into a crystal ball and enter a meditative trance that would open the subconscious, revealing psychic information about the past, present, or future. Celebrate one of witchcraft's most iconic tools with this cocktail, allowing the honey and lavender to open your psychic abilities and protect you in your mystical travels!

TOOLS: citrus juicer, 2 small dishes, coupe glass, cocktail shaker, strainer

1 tablespoon sugar	**½ ounce triple sec**
1 teaspoon honey	**Juice of ½ lemon**
1½ ounces brandy	**1 dash orange bitters**
¾ ounce Honey-Lavender	**1 lemon wheel**
Simple Syrup (page 20)	

Pour the sugar into a small dish, and drizzle the honey into another small dish. Dip a coupe glass rim into the honey, then into the sugar to coat. Fill a cocktail shaker with ice, and pour in the brandy, simple syrup, triple sec, and lemon juice. Add the bitters. Cover and shake. Strain the drink into the prepared glass, and garnish with the lemon wheel.

> **SPELL / RITUAL:** *Sit in a darkened room with a crystal ball or a translucent crystal. Imagine your third eye (at the center of your forehead) expanding. Gently gaze into the ball while opening your mind to whatever images or patterns come to you. Practice this ritual multiple times to become clearer and more confident in what you see!*

Spellbinding Swap: Swap out the brandy for vodka.

Samhain Spirits

Samhain (also known as Halloween) is the beginning and ending of the witches' New Year! On this day, it is thought that the veil between the physical world and the spirit world is particularly thin. What better time to connect with your spiritual side?! Brew up this bangin' potion to celebrate this special day as you reflect on the past year and call in the energy of the year ahead.

TOOLS: 2 small dishes, rocks glass, cocktail shaker, bar spoon

1 tablespoon honey
1 tablespoon ground cinnamon
3 ounces espresso, cooled

1½ ounces peanut butter whiskey
1½ ounces pumpkin liqueur
¾ ounce crème de menthe
2 dashes vanilla extract

Pour the honey into a small dish, and place the cinnamon in another small dish. Dip a rocks glass rim into the honey, then into the cinnamon to coat. Fill a cocktail shaker with ice, and pour in the espresso, peanut butter whiskey, pumpkin liqueur, crème de menthe, and vanilla. Stir to mix. Pour into the prepared rocks glass.

SPELL / RITUAL: *Assemble your coven in the moonlight. Pour salt in a giant spiral, then place a candle and a handful of nuts—symbolizing new beginnings and growth—in the center. Hold hands in a circle, and walk inward toward the center of the spiral, mentally leaving behind something from the past year. Once you get to the center, light the candle, and have each person take a nut as they walk out of the spiral, thinking about their intentions for the coming year.*

Spellbinding Swap: Not a fan of whiskey? Swap it out for vodka.

BEER

GIN

The Brewster

Think crafting beer is mainly for dudes? Think again! In the Dark Ages, women who brewed beer were called brewsters. Known for wearing pointy hats so they would be noticed in a crowded marketplace, brewsters placed broomsticks over doorways of the local ale house to let patrons know when the brew was ready. To protect their ingredients, brewsters kept cats in the brewhouses to safeguard their grains from rodents. Mix up this effervescent elixir, and raise a glass to the trailblazing brewsters!

TOOLS: citrus juicer, cocktail shaker, bar spoon, tulip glass, strainer

6 ounces light lager (such as Heineken)
1½ ounces gin
1 ounce Aperol

1½ ounces freshly squeezed grapefruit juice
1 orange wedge

Fill a cocktail shaker with ice, and pour in the beer, gin, Aperol, and grapefruit juice. Stir gently. Fill a tulip glass with ice, then strain the drink into it. Garnish with the orange wedge.

SPELL / RITUAL: *As you pour the beer into your cocktail shaker, repeat these words: I celebrate and honor the brewsters, the trailblazers who brewed with love. May their memories live on as they smile from above.*

Spellbinding Swap: If you don't have Aperol, use Campari or Pimm's No. 1 instead.

Selene's Secret

Selene, whose name means "light," is the Greek goddess of the moon—though some believe she IS the moon. Craft this magical cocktail, and connect with Selene as she sheds light upon you, illuminating any mysteries that are on your path.

TOOLS: saucepan, wooden spoon, muddler, 2 small dishes, Irish coffee mug, strainer

12 ounces water
1 herbal green tea bag
4 teaspoons ground cinnamon, divided
3 whole cloves
1 orange slice
2 tablespoons honey, divided
2 tablespoons sugar

In a small saucepan, combine the water, tea bag, 2 teaspoons of cinnamon, the cloves, orange slice, and 1 tablespoon of honey. Bring to a boil over high heat while stirring with a wooden spoon and muddling the orange. Remove from the heat. Pour the remaining 1 tablespoon of honey into a small dish. In another small dish, combine the sugar and remaining 2 teaspoons of cinnamon. Dip the rim of an Irish coffee mug into the honey, then into the cinnamon sugar to coat. Strain the hot drink into the mug.

SPELL / RITUAL: *Lay down a white cloth, and place a moonstone, selenite, or item made of silver on it. Declare this an offering to Selene, then sit with her, and feel her strength. Ask her to open your intuition and shed light on an area of your life for which you wish to receive insight.*

Batch It: Multiply the recipe by the number of drinks needed. Rim the appropriate number of glasses, and set aside. Bring the ingredients to a boil, then strain into the prepared mugs.

Midnight Magic

Our parents used to say nothing good happens after midnight, but we disagree! Midnight has a special kind of energy and can be the perfect time to celebrate successes, milestones, and spiritual growth. Cherries symbolize rebirth and renewal, making this tasty potion a perfect addition to any celebration!

TOOLS: flute glass, bar spoon

3 ounces dark rum
½ ounce Amaretto

6 ounces cherry-flavored cola or regular cola
Cherries, for garnish

Fill a flute glass with ice. Pour in the rum, then add the Amaretto. Top with the cola, and gently stir to mix. Garnish with cherries.

SPELL / RITUAL: *Raise your glass as the clock strikes midnight, and repeat these words: I celebrate me, and so will it be.*

Spellbinding Swap: Don't have cherry cola on hand? Use regular cola, and add ½ ounce cherry juice.

Sixth Sense

Tapping into your basic five senses is soooo last season. Cultivate your sixth sense with basil, which enhances your mental abilities, making it perfect for spiritual work and growth. Brew this potion when you're looking for a little extra help connecting to the spirit world.

TOOLS: citrus juicer, paring knife, cocktail shaker, muddler, strainer, martini glass

1 basil sprig, plus a basil flower or leaf for garnish
Juice of ½ lemon
3 ounces bourbon
¾ ounce Aperol
¾ ounce Classic Simple Syrup (page 20)
1 orange peel

In a cocktail shaker, muddle the basil and lemon juice. Pour in the bourbon, Aperol, and simple syrup. Fill the shaker with ice, cover, and shake. Strain the drink into a martini glass. Garnish with the orange peel and a basil flower or leaf.

SPELL / RITUAL: *Oracle cards are a tool to help you receive messages from your higher self and your spiritual guides. Sit with your oracle card deck, center and ground yourself, and ask a question—or simply ask the deck this question: "What is it I need to know today?" Hold the question in your mind as you shuffle the cards. Pull a card, and enjoy pondering and pontificating the message of the card and how it relates to you.*

Spellbinding Swap: Swap out the bourbon for any kind of whiskey.

Mother Earth

Connecting with Mother Earth and the natural world around us is an essential part of witchcraft. Mother Earth represents abundance and resources, providing us with energy, food, shelter, and magic. The blueberries in this potion will help connect you with the energy of abundance, making it the perfect cocktail to give thanks for all you have received.

TOOLS: citrus juicer, cocktail shaker, muddler, wine glass

13 fresh blueberries
1 fresh strawberry
Juice of ½ lime
3 ounces white rum

¾ ounce Classic Simple
Syrup (page 20)
1 ounce pasteurized egg
whites

Fill a cocktail shaker with ice. Add 10 blueberries, the strawberry, and lime juice, and muddle together. Pour in the rum, simple syrup, and egg whites. Cover and shake until frothy. Pour the drink into a wine glass, and float the remaining 3 blueberries on top.

SPELL / RITUAL: *Light a candle, and repeat the following words: Abundance flows to me every day and in every way. I recognize and appreciate all the gifts I have received in my life thus far. I am open and receptive to receiving more of what I truly need.*

Spellbinding Swap: Omit the eggs if desired.

Mystify Me

There's literally nothing we love more than diving into life's most mystifying topics—just ask anyone who has listened to our *Mystify Me* podcast! Thinking about life's biggest questions can feel overwhelming, but we find that it's all about staying open, remaining curious, and seeing what resonates to help you live your best life. So, pour yourself a cocktail, jump on the *Mystify Me* podcast train, and travel down the mystical rabbit hole with us!

TOOLS: citrus juicer, cocktail shaker, strainer, martini glass

Juice of ¾ orange
Juice of ½ lemon
Juice of ½ lime
4½ ounces white rum

1½ ounces blue curaçao
½ ounce agave nectar
1 purple rock candy stick

In a cocktail shaker, combine the orange, lemon, and lime juices. Add ice to the shaker, then pour in the rum, blue curaçao, and agave. Cover and shake well, then strain the drink into a martini glass. Garnish with the rock candy, stirring at will!

SPELL / RITUAL: *Make thinking about mystifying topics a part of your daily life! Ponder the spiritual world while taking a walk or doing daily tasks like cooking or driving. Listen to spiritually enlightening podcasts, audiobooks, or guided meditations. Don't know where to start? We love Many Lives, Many Masters by Brian Weiss, Michael Newton's Journey of Souls, the Almost 30 podcast, and of course, the Mystify Me podcast with yours truly!*

Batch It: Have a *Mystify Me* podcast listening party with your coven! Batch this recipe by multiplying the recipe by the number of drinks needed.

The Athena

Athena and cranberries make a powerful pair! The majestic Athena is the ideal goddess to call upon when you need a little extra support as you travel along your spiritual and healing path. In this libation, we also utilize cranberries' ability to heal while supporting your mental and spiritual well-being.

TOOLS: blender, small dish, tulip glass

1½ ounces vodka	**½ teaspoon honey**
3 fresh strawberries	**2 ounces sparkling water**
2 fresh sage leaves	**2 lime wedges**
1½ ounces cranberry juice	

In a blender, combine the vodka, strawberries, sage, and cranberry juice. Blend well. Pour the honey into a small dish, then dip the rim of a tulip glass into the honey to coat, and carefully fill the glass with ice. Pour the drink into the glass, leaving room at the top. Add the sparkling water. Squeeze a lime wedge into the drink, and garnish with the second.

SPELL / RITUAL: *Make a spell jar. Set an intention for well-being, then fill a small jar with magical healing ingredients. We suggest infusing salt, lavender, dried cranberries, dried sage, dried rosemary, and small clear quartz crystals with a healing intention. Once you have infused your ingredients, seal the jar with wax, and decorate it. Meditate with your jar, and find a special place for it to live.*

Mocktail Magic: Omit the vodka.

The Mermaid

Mermaids embody divine feminine energy and, like witches, are known for their fierce individuality. These magical beings are seen as wise and uniquely in tune with the world around them. If mermaids had a mantra, it would be "go with the flow," encouraging us to relax into the natural ebbs and flows of life. Embrace your inner mermaid with this recipe as you surrender to divine timing and the infinite wisdom of the Universe.

TOOLS: cocktail shaker, muddler, bar spoon, tulip glass, strainer

1 (2-inch) piece watermelon
6 fresh blueberries
4 fresh mint leaves
3 ounces white wine

¾ ounce triple sec
2 dashes lemon bitters
1 blue rock candy stick

In a cocktail shaker, muddle the watermelon, blueberries, and mint. Pour in the wine and triple sec, then add the bitters. Stir. Fill a tulip glass with ice, then strain the drink into it. Garnish with the rock candy.

SPELL / RITUAL: *Immerse yourself in a bathtub, shower, or natural body of water. Pay attention to the way the water flows around you. Just as river water flows around a large rock, imagine that you are flowing around any challenges (rocks) in your life gracefully and effortlessly.*

Spellbinding Swap: Try vodka or rum instead of wine.

The Money Maker

Get that money, honey! Money is a physical expression of energy, and as such, it constantly flows and shifts. When we act from a place of scarcity or lack, always thinking we do not have enough, we can unknowingly create energetic blocks to abundance. Let this potion help you clear any blocks, so you can stay in a space of abundance and allow the energy of money to flow freely to you.

TOOLS: cocktail shaker, bar spoon, strainer, chilled martini glass

2 ounces vodka
2 ounces lemonade
½ ounce Honey-Lavender
  Simple Syrup (page 20)

Splash sparkling water
1 thyme sprig

Fill a cocktail shaker with ice, and pour in the vodka honey-lavender simple syrup, and lemonade. Stir gently, then strain the drink into a chilled martini glass. Top with sparkling water, and garnish with the thyme sprig.

SPELL / RITUAL: *Repeat the following words: Money flows to me easily and effortlessly. I am open to and worthy of receiving financial abundance in all its forms. I am now aligned with and can recognize the opportunities that will lead me to a life of financial abundance and freedom.*

Mocktail Magic: Omit the vodka, and increase the amount of lemonade.

The Spicy Ginger

You are no basic witch, babe! Embrace your fiery ginger within as you enjoy this fierce concoction. Ginger is a powerhouse herb, offering magical properties that enhance sensuality and self-confidence. Not only does ginger open you up to adventure and new journeys, but it also accelerates magic—which means it's a perfect partner to work on those pressing matters!

TOOLS: small dish, martini glass, cocktail shaker, muddler, strainer

1 teaspoon ginger salt
¼ fresh jalapeño (seeded if you're sensitive to heat)
1 (1¼-inch) piece fresh ginger, peeled and chopped

1½ ounces gin
1½ ounces vodka
2 dashes orange bitters
¾ ounce ginger beer

Spread the ginger salt in a small dish. Dip the rim of a martini glass into water, then into the salt to coat. In a cocktail shaker, muddle the jalapeño and ginger. Pour in the gin and vodka, then add the bitters and ice. Cover and shake well, then strain the drink into the prepared glass. Top with the ginger beer.

SPELL / RITUAL: *To support spiritual growth, chew on a piece of fresh ginger while spellcasting and potion-making, letting the aroma and flavor inspire courage and confidence.*

Spellbinding Swap: Swap in table or sea salt for the ginger salt.

Karmic Boost

They say karma's a b*tch—or is it a boost? Spiritual growth is all about being able to identify and work on your karmic lessons. Call upon the orange in this recipe to enhance your ability to recognize karmic patterns, change those patterns for the better, and improve your karmic vibration!

TOOLS: citrus juicer, blender, pint glass, fine-mesh sieve, cocktail shaker

1 tablespoon honey
½ orange, peeled
4 fresh mint leaves
2 ounces tequila

Juice of 1 lime
Juice of ½ lemon
1 orange slice

In a blender, combine the honey, orange, mint, and tequila. Blend until the honey is dissolved. Fill a pint glass with ice. Using a fine-mesh sieve, strain the mixture into the glass. Pour in the lime juice and lemon juice. Cover the glass with a cocktail shaker, and gently shake to combine. Garnish the edge of the glass with the orange slice.

SPELL / RITUAL: *Halve an orange. Place 5 drops of frankincense essential oil and 5 drops of myrrh essential oil onto one orange half. Close your eyes, take a few deep breaths to inhale the aroma, and connect to spirit. Reflect on any current challenges in your life, and ask your guides to shine light on the karmic lesson attached to those challenges. Allow any visions, messages, or feelings to come to you.*

Mocktail Magic: Omit the tequila.

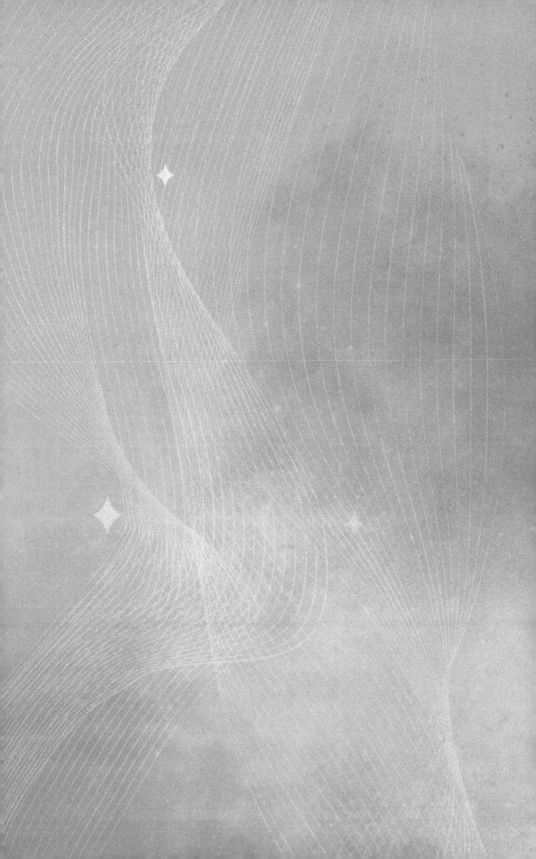

7

STRENGTH & BOUNDARIES

The Philosopher's Stone   119

Lilith's Power   120

The Night Terror   121

Protection Potion   122

Justice for Witches   123

Defense against the Dark Arts   124

The Split   125

Blackberry Magic   126

The Guardian   127

The Firefly   128

The Evil Eye   129

Repellent   130

Eviction Notice   131

Virginal Sacrifice   132

The Shield   133

◆ Trial by Fire   134

Unleash your source of personal power! Magical self-care includes connecting with your inner warrior for strength while also setting strong and healthy boundaries. This chapter includes topics like enhancing spiritual strength, cord cutting, and protecting yourself and your home against negativity. Don't ever forget that you are one powerful, badass witch!

The Philosopher's Stone

Legend has it that the philosopher's stone was a substance that could turn ordinary metals, such as iron, lead, nickel, and copper, into gold. It also acted as a powerful potion that could cure illness, reawaken the properties of youth, and grant immortality to those who possessed it. Be your own philosopher's stone with this elixir, and turn challenging situations into a source of personal strength!

TOOLS: citrus juicer, vegetable peeler, cocktail shaker, bar spoon, rocks glass

1½ ounces bourbon
1½ ounces sweet tea vodka
1 ounce triple sec
Juice of ½ lemon

2 teaspoons agave nectar
1 lemon twist
Edible gold leaf (optional)

Fill a cocktail shaker with ice, and pour in the bourbon, vodka, triple sec, lemon juice, and agave. Stir, and pour into a rocks glass. Garnish with the lemon twist and a pinch of edible gold leaf (if using).

SPELL / RITUAL: *Fire is the ultimate transformer. Write down a current challenge or difficult situation on a piece of paper. Light the paper on fire, and repeat these words: By the light of this fire, I turn darkness into light. May this light illuminate me, and may I radiate wisdom and strength.*

Spellbinding Swap: If you don't have sweet tea vodka, use regular vodka with iced tea, or omit the tea.

Lilith's Power

Known as the dark moon goddess, Lilith has been worshipped as the ruler of both light and dark. Storied for liberating herself from Adam and initiating the first divorce, she is the perfect goddess to help you harness your inner feminine strength. Create this cocktail to call upon Lilith and face your fears with bravery and beauty. Cinnamon is known for its magical ability to enhance personal power. And let's be real, if Lilith were going to make herself a drink, it'd be whiskey . . . because she's badass. This recipe makes enough for two.

TOOLS: paring knife, 2 rocks glasses, bar spoon

8 teaspoons Cinnamon-Rosemary Simple Syrup (page 20)

4 dashes orange bitters

4 ounces whiskey

2 orange peels

In a rocks glass, combine 4 teaspoons of simple syrup and 2 dashes of orange bitters. Swirl to coat the inside of the glass. Add ice, then add 2 ounces of whiskey and 1 orange peel. Stir. Repeat this process for the second drink.

> SPELL / RITUAL: *As an offering to Lilith, make her a cocktail first. Once you both have a cocktail, close your eyes, and speak these words:* Lilith, please ignite my spiritual strength and resiliency from deep inside. I am now empowered to face my fears and challenges with the confidence, poise, and will of a goddess.

Spellbinding Swap: Swap out the Cinnamon-Rosemary Simple Syrup for Classic Simple Syrup (page 20).

The Night Terror

Everyone gets nightmares from time to time, but don't allow them to get you down! Keep those bad dreams at bay with this magical elixir. The chamomile, lemon balm, and lavender will relax your mind and call in a peaceful sleep full of lovely, charmed dreams.

TOOLS: saucepan, fine-mesh sieve, Irish coffee mug, bar spoon

12 ounces water
1 chamomile tea bag
1 lemon balm tea bag
1 teaspoon dried
  culinary-grade lavender,
  plus more for garnish

1 ounce Honey-Lavender
  Simple Syrup (page 20)
2 ounces whiskey
1 lemon wedge

In a small saucepan, combine the water, chamomile tea bag, lemon balm tea bag, and lavender. Bring to a boil over high heat, then reduce the heat to low. Simmer for 5 minutes. Remove from the heat. Using a fine-mesh sieve, strain the mixture into an Irish coffee mug, then stir in the simple syrup and whiskey. Squeeze the lemon wedge into the cocktail. Sprinkle a few lavender buds on top.

SPELL / RITUAL: *Place a smoky quartz next to your bed. Ask it to protect you from any negative influences that may contribute to bad dreams.*

Mocktail Magic: Omit the whiskey.

Protection Potion

Protect yourself before you wreck yourself! Both cranberry and lime are known for being superior protectors. This is the perfect potion to conjure up when you're feeling vulnerable or under attack.

TOOLS: citrus juicer, cocktail shaker, bar spoon, strainer, flute glass

4 ounces vodka
1 ounce cranberry juice
¾ ounce Vanilla Bean Simple
  Syrup (page 20)

½ ounce freshly squeezed
  lime juice
1 ounce sparkling water
3 fresh cranberries

Fill a cocktail shaker with ice, and pour in the vodka, cranberry juice, simple syrup, and lime juice. Stir, then strain the drink into a flute glass. Top with the sparkling water, and garnish with the cranberries.

SPELL / RITUAL: *One by one, drop in each cranberry while repeating these words: I am strong. I will not absorb any energy that is not my own. I am protected. I am loved.*

Mocktail Magic: Omit the vodka, and add more cranberry juice and sparkling water.

Justice for Witches

Hang on while we climb onto our soapbox for a second! During the witch trials in Europe and the United States, tens of thousands of people were put to death. Witch hunting is still happening in modern times. Thousands are executed due to witch hunting–related violence each year. Allow the cola in this elixir, made from the kola nut, to bring peace to this harrowing situation. If you feel drawn to do so, visit Witch-Hunt.org while sipping on this delicious libation to learn more and how to help.

TOOLS: Collins glass, bar spoon

1½ ounces dark rum
½ ounce triple sec
3 dashes Angostura bitters

5 ounces cola, plus more as needed
1 Maraschino cherry

Fill a Collins glass with ice. Pour in the rum and triple sec, then add the bitters. Top with the cola to taste. Stir well, and garnish with the cherry.

> SPELL / RITUAL: *Light a black candle for protection and a white candle for purification and peace. Send protective light to all who practice witchcraft or healing work. Imagine them surrounded in a white or silver light, being guided, shielded, and supported.*

Spellbinding Swap: Substitute whiskey for the rum.

Defense against the Dark Arts

Did you know that blueberries are magically utilized as a psychic protection tool?! When casting spells or practicing any spiritual work, it is imperative that you also hone protection practices and skills. This potion will help shield you from any negative energies, intentions, or influences that may interfere with your highest good.

TOOLS: cocktail shaker, muddler, Collins glass, strainer

20 fresh blueberries
1 (2-inch) watermelon cube
3 fresh cilantro leaves

1½ ounces white rum
3 ounces sparkling water
1 cilantro sprig

In a cocktail shaker, muddle 12 blueberries, the watermelon, cilantro, and rum. Fill a Collins glass with ice, and strain the drink into it. Top with the sparkling water. Garnish with the remaining 8 blueberries and cilantro sprig.

SPELL / RITUAL: *Raise your glass, and repeat these words three times: Protection comes this way; may all negativity be banished this day. So mote it be.*

Mocktail Magic: Omit the rum, and increase the amount of sparkling water.

The Split

This is a split that everyone can do! Did you know that coffee's magical healing properties include establishing strength and boundaries and helping disconnect from toxic situations? Call on coffee when you are ready to cut energetic cords or ties to people or if you need support with challenging situations that you are ready to move on from.

TOOLS: blender, tall beer mug

2 ounces peanut butter
  whiskey
2 ounces banana whiskey
2 ounces coffee liqueur
1 ounce Irish cream liqueur

1 (3-inch) slice banana
1 teaspoon ground cinnamon
3 coffee beans (regular or
  chocolate covered)

In a blender, combine the peanut butter whiskey, banana whiskey, coffee liqueur, Irish cream liqueur, and banana. Add enough ice to fill. Blend well, and pour into a tall beer mug. Sprinkle the cinnamon on top, and garnish with the coffee beans.

SPELL / RITUAL: *Inscribe your name on one candle and another person's name (or situation) on another candle. Tie a piece of string around the two candles, light the candles, and place a tealight under the string. Light the tealight. As the heat from the tealight burns the string and it breaks, allow the energetic tie to be broken. Feel gratitude and a sense of freedom.*

Batch It: Multiply the recipe by the number of drinks needed.

GIN

WINE

Blackberry Magic

Considered a shielding plant for more than just its sharp thorns, the blackberry bush is commonly used for physical and spiritual protection. Blackberry leaves have been used to dress wounds to safeguard against excessive bleeding and infection. In addition, blackberries are used for spiritual protection against malevolent energies, vampires, shadow witches, and other dark energies.

TOOLS: paring knife, cocktail shaker, muddler, bar spoon, strainer, chilled martini glass, cocktail spear

6 fresh blackberries
3 ounces gin
1½ ounces white wine

¾ ounce Classic Simple
  Syrup (page 20)
1 tablespoon honey
1 lemon peel

Fill a cocktail shaker one-third full with ice. Add 3 blackberries, and muddle them. Pour in the gin, wine, simple syrup, and honey. Stir until well mixed. Strain the drink into a chilled martini glass, and garnish with the lemon peel and remaining 3 blackberries, speared.

SPELL / RITUAL: *Combine charcoal, salt, white sage, and blackberry leaves. Sprinkle this protection spell around the exterior perimeter of your home or near your home's entrances to ward off negative intentions or energies.*

Batch It: Multiply the recipe by the number of drinks needed. In a pitcher, muddle the blackberries. Stir in the next four ingredients until well mixed. Pour into chilled martini glasses, and garnish with lemon peel.

The Guardian

Ginger, one of the first spices imported to Europe, has become one of the most powerful healing herbs in a witch's cabinet. Ginger can be used to treat physical ailments such as colds, indigestion, inflammation, menstrual pain, nausea, and a host of other issues. On a spiritual level, ginger's magical properties include invoking love, luck, protection, and success and replenishing your magical energy. With its uber-powerful healing properties for body, mind, and spirit, this is just the right recipe when you need a little extra support or protection. We love this drink any time our batteries feel low!

TOOLS: citrus juicer, cocktail shaker, bar spoon, tulip glass

Juice of 1 lime
¾ ounce Classic Simple Syrup (page 20)
3 ounces ginger ale
3 ounces ginger beer

6 ounces light lager (such as Heineken)
1 slice fresh or candied ginger
1 lime wheel

In a cocktail shaker, combine the lime juice, simple syrup, ginger ale, ginger beer, and lager. Stir gently. Fill a tulip glass with ice, and pour the drink into it. Garnish with the ginger slice and lime wheel.

SPELL / RITUAL: *Chew the ginger garnish, savoring the flavor, texture, and aroma of this magical spice. Repeat the following words aloud or in your mind: I call on my spirit guides to bring me the highest level of protection from all negative influences or energies that surround me, known and unknown. May my physical, mental, emotional, and spiritual body be grounded, centered, and protected in accordance with my highest self.*

Mocktail Magic: Swap out the light beer for a non-alcoholic beer.

The Firefly

Associated with the element of fire, cayenne is a must-have for witches, as it brings strength, motivation, courage, and protection. It is a powerful tool for repelling negativity, breaking curses or hexes, and warding off evil spirits. It is also said to expand your aura and protect you from absorbing the energy of others.

TOOLS: citrus juicer, cocktail shaker, strainer, coupe glass

2 ounces tequila
½ ounce Classic Simple
  Syrup (page 20)
Juice of 1 lime
Juice of ½ lemon
¾ ounce cranberry juice

¾ ounce pasteurized
  egg whites
3 dashes orange bitters
¼ teaspoon cayenne, plus
  more for garnish

Fill a cocktail shaker halfway with ice. Pour in the tequila, simple syrup, lime juice, lemon juice, cranberry juice, and egg whites. Add the bitters and cayenne. Cover and shake vigorously, then strain the drink into a coupe glass. Garnish with a sprinkle of cayenne.

SPELL / RITUAL: *Just as fireflies use their light to ward off predators, use a candle or flashlight to fill your energy field with protection and banish any darkness. Hold the light in your hands, and imagine a strong, benevolent light expanding and surrounding you. Envision the light pulling out any negative energy you may have absorbed from the world. Want to make it more potent? Fireflies magnify their presence by flashing in unison—and so can you! Call in your besties, sit in a circle, and create a sphere of protection as you each hold a light.*

Spellbinding Swap: Swap out the simple syrup for honey, maple syrup, or agave nectar.

The Evil Eye

Our protective twist on this classic dirty martini features rosemary for its magical ability to drive away negative influences. Create this drink to expel any person or energies in your life that are sending *dirty* (not the fun kind) vibes your way. You will banish negative influences in your life, and this powerhouse cocktail also features olives, which represent friendship and peace. We love to sip this martini as we banish evil and darkness with love and light.

TOOLS: martini glass, cocktail shaker, bar spoon, strainer

4½ ounces vodka	**3 olives**
¾ ounce dry vermouth	**1 rosemary sprig**
¾ ounce olive brine	

Chill a martini glass with ice. Fill a cocktail shaker halfway with ice, and pour in the vodka, vermouth, and olive brine. Stir gently until well chilled. Strain the drink into the chilled martini glass. Garnish with 2 olives, speared onto the rosemary sprig. Reserve the last olive for the spell.

> SPELL / RITUAL: *With a hand over your heart, repeat this spell:*
> *My path now separates from negative people, places, projects, and energies. I thank these sources for the lessons and growth they provided. I now walk the path that leads me to love, light, friendship, and peace. So mote it be. Drop an olive in the martini glass, and enjoy your new beginning.*

Spellbinding Swap: If you don't have a rosemary sprig, use a cocktail spear.

Repellent

Sometimes you've gotta repel more than mosquitos! Spiritually, lemons are used to absorb negative energy and cleanse the aura. Think of lemons as a negative energy bug repellent!

TOOLS: zester, citrus juicer, small dish, martini glass, cocktail shaker, strainer

1 tablespoon sugar	Juice of ½ lemon
Grated zest of ½ lemon	¾ ounce Classic Simple
1 lemon wedge	Syrup (page 20)
3 ounces citrus vodka	4 ounces pink lemonade
¾ ounce triple sec	5 lemon wheels

In a small dish, combine the sugar and lemon zest. Rub the zest into the sugar with your fingers until the mixture turns a yellow hue. Wet the rim of a martini glass with the lemon wedge, then dip the rim into the lemon sugar to coat. Fill a cocktail shaker with ice, and pour in the vodka, triple sec, lemon juice, simple syrup, and lemonade. Cover and shake well, then strain the drink into the prepared martini glass. Garnish with 1 lemon wheel, saving the rest for the spell.

SPELL / RITUAL: *While sipping this refreshing and protective cocktail, place the remaining lemon wheels around your house to repel any negative or unwanted energy. Take caution to keep away from pets if they live in the home with you.*

Spellbinding Swap: Swap out citrus vodka for regular vodka.

Eviction Notice

Bad vibes, be gone! If you sense something negative in your home, it is time to give it the spiritual boot with this powerful potion and spell. Blackberries are known in witchcraft for their protective qualities and may be used to remove evil spirits from a home, protecting against anyone doing you harm.

TOOLS: citrus juicer, Collins glass, muddler

3 fresh mint leaves
1½ ounces white rum
½ ounce Blackberry Simple Syrup (page 20)

½ ounce freshly squeezed lemon juice
½ ounce sparkling water
1 mint sprig

In a Collins glass, muddle the mint leaves. Pour in the rum, simple syrup, and lemon juice. Add ice, and top with the sparkling water. Garnish with the mint sprig.

> SPELL / RITUAL: *Apples are known as a spiritual protection tool for banishing negative energy. Cut 4 apples through the middle to expose the pentagram inside. Place the apples around your home (take caution to keep away from pets if they live in the home with you), and sprinkle blackberry leaves on them to tell any negative energy it's time to go!*

Mocktail Magic: Replace the rum with cranberry juice.

Virginal Sacrifice

Sometimes you just want to put some boundaries around alcohol consumption. This is our favorite "almost" virgin drink. Call upon the pineapple in this concoction to conjure up self-assurance and confidence, which can be especially helpful in pressure-filled social situations.

TOOLS: cocktail shaker, bar spoon, margarita glass

6 dashes Angostura bitters　　**1 lime wedge**
2 ounces pineapple juice　　**6 ounces tonic water**

Fill a cocktail shaker with ice, add the bitters, cover, and shake. Pour in the pineapple juice, then squeeze in the lime wedge. Top with the tonic water, stir gently, and slowly pour into a margarita glass. Garnish with a paper umbrella if desired.

SPELL / RITUAL: *Place a hematite crystal in your pocket, bra, or purse to bring forth your sense of inner power. This is especially helpful in situations with social pressure that may not be aligned with your personal goals.*

Spellbinding Swap: Add 1½ ounces vodka or gin to make this a cocktail!

The Shield

When life gets tough, create your own shield! Lemons are excellent for cleansing and removing negative energy blockages, and sage is a top-notch protector. This potion is designed to help you walk through the world with confidence and freedom.

TOOLS: citrus juicer, cocktail shaker, strainer, chilled rocks glass

1½ ounces brandy
1 ounce freshly squeezed lemon juice

1 ounce crème de cassis
3 fresh sage leaves

Fill a cocktail shaker with ice, and pour in the brandy, lemon juice, and crème de cassis. Cover and shake, then strain the drink into a chilled rocks glass. Garnish with 1 sage leaf, and use the remaining leaves in the spell.

SPELL / RITUAL: *While holding a sage leaf in each hand, close your eyes, and envision a protective shield of light radiating from your heart center, enveloping your mind, body, and spirit in a strong and protective armor. Place the sage under your pillow for continued protection.*

Spellbinding Swap: Swap out the crème de cassis for triple sec.

Trial by Fire

It's believed that the phrase "trial by fire" originated during the Salem Witch Trials in Massachusetts. Today, we use this phrase to describe a person's ability to excel under pressure. When you've found yourself thrown into the metaphorical fire of life, prepare this potion to conjure up your inner strength.

TOOLS: paring knife, saucepan, small dish, Irish coffee mug

6 ounces water

1 tablespoon honey

2 lemon slices

1 cinnamon stick

1 tablespoon sugar

1 tablespoon ground cinnamon

2 ounces Cognac

Lemon peel, for flaming (see page 21)

In a small saucepan, combine the water, honey, lemon slices, and cinnamon stick. Bring to a boil over high heat. Remove from the heat, and cover the pan with a lid. Steep for 5 to 10 minutes. In a small dish, combine the sugar and cinnamon. Wet the rim of an Irish coffee mug with water, then dip it into the cinnamon sugar to coat. Pour the hot drink into the mug, and add the Cognac. Flame the lemon peel over the drink to finish.

SPELL / RITUAL: *In a small jar, combine cinnamon, dried bay leaves, dried sage, dried sunflower seeds, sunstone, and tiger's eye crystal chips. Place the lid on the jar, and use a flame to melt green wax over the lid to seal it with good luck. Carry the spell jar with you in your pocket or purse to walk through any situation with strength and courage.*

Spellbinding Swap: Swap in whiskey for the Cognac.

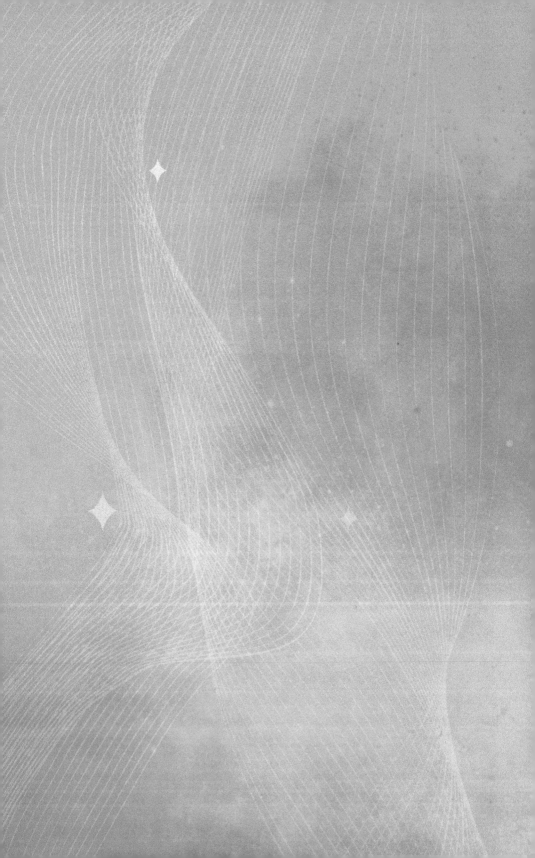

MEASUREMENT CONVERSIONS

VOLUME EQUIVALENTS

	U.S. STANDARD	U.S. STANDARD (OUNCES)	METRIC (APPROXIMATE)
LIQUID	2 tablespoons	1 fl. oz.	30 mL
	¼ cup	2 fl. oz.	60 mL
	½ cup	4 fl. oz.	120 mL
	1 cup	8 fl. oz.	240 mL
	1½ cups	12 fl. oz.	355 mL
	2 cups or 1 pint	16 fl. oz.	475 mL
	4 cups or 1 quart	32 fl. oz.	1 L
	1 gallon	128 fl. oz.	4 L
DRY	⅛ teaspoon	–	0.5 mL
	¼ teaspoon	–	1 mL
	½ teaspoon	–	2 mL
	¾ teaspoon	–	4 mL
	1 teaspoon	–	5 mL
	1 tablespoon	–	15 mL
	¼ cup	–	59 mL
	⅓ cup	–	79 mL
	½ cup	–	118 mL
	⅔ cup	–	156 mL
	¾ cup	–	177 mL
	1 cup	–	235 mL
	2 cups or 1 pint	–	475 mL
	3 cups	–	700 mL
	4 cups or 1 quart	–	1 L
	½ gallon	–	2 L
	1 gallon	–	4 L

REFERENCES

Calabrese, Salvatore. *The Complete Home Bartender's Guide: Tools, Ingredients, Techniques, and Recipes for the Perfect Drink.* New York City: Sterling Publishing, 2019.

Cunningham, Scott. *Cunningham's Encyclopedia of Magical Herbs.* Woodbury, MN: Llewellyn Publications, 1985.

Hadas, Julia Halina. *WitchCraft Cocktails: 70 Seasonal Drinks Infused with Magic and Ritual.* Avon, MA: Adams Media, 2020.

Mankey, Jason. *Witch's Wheel of the Year: Rituals for Circles, Solitaries, and Covens.* Woodbury, MN: Llewellyn Publications, 2017.

Meehan, Jim, and Chris Gall. *The PDT Cocktail Book: The Complete Bartender's Guide from the Celebrated Speakeasy.* New York City: Sterling Publishing, 2011.

Miernowska, Marysia. *The Witch's Herbal Apothecary: Rituals and Recipes for a Year of Earth Magick and Sacred Medicine Making.* Beverly, MA: Quarto Publishing Group, 2020.

Murphy-Hiscock, Arin. *Protection Spells: Clear Negative Energy, Banish Unhealthy Influences, and Embrace Your Power.* Avon, MA: Adams Media, 2018.

Murphy-Hiscock, Arin. *The Green Witch: Your Complete Guide to the Natural Magic of Herbs, Flowers, Essential Oils, and More.* Avon, MA: Adams Media, 2017.

Pamita, Madame. *The Book of Candle Magic: Candle Spell Secrets to Change Your Life.* Woodbury, MN: Llewellyn Publications, 2020.

Regan, Gary. *The Joy of Mixology, Revised and Updated Edition: The Consummate Guide to the Bartender's Craft.* New York City: Clarkson Potter, 2018.

Robbins, Shawn, and Charity Bedell. *The Good Witch's Guide: A Modern-Day Wiccapedia of Magickal Ingredients and Spells.* New York City: Sterling Publishing, 2017.

Robbins, Shawn, and Leanna Greenaway. *Wiccapedia: A Modern-Day White Witch's Guide.* New York City: Sterling Publishing, 2014.

Stewart, Amy. *The Drunken Botanist.* Chapel Hill, NC: Algonquin Books, 2013.

INDEX

A

All Hallows' Eve, 61
Amaretto
  Midnight Magic, 106
  Pop My Cherry, 48
  The Seductress, 51
The Amethyst, 91
The Athena, 110
Autumn Equinox, 30
Autumn Equinox (cocktail), 99

B

Basil, 14
  The Magic Wand, 79
  Sixth Sense, 107
  Summer Solstice (cocktail), 69
Beer
  The Brewster, 104
  The Cauldron, 50
  Cupid's Cauldron, 42
  Eclipse, 64
  The Guardian, 127
  Light & Love, 80
  Wicked Sexy Witch, 83
Berries, 14
  Autumn Equinox (cocktail), 99
  The Athena, 110
  Berry Brew, 89
  Blackberry Magic, 126
  Blackberry Simple Syrup, 20

Defense against the Dark
  Arts, 124
  Light & Love, 80
  Mercury Retrograde, 60
  The Mermaid, 111
  Mother Earth, 108
  Protection Potion, 122
  Strawberry Moon, 68
  Strawberry Simple Syrup, 20
  Summer Solstice (cocktail), 69
  Wicked Sexy Witch, 83
Bewitching Beauty, 86
Bitters, 16
  The Amethyst, 91
  Crystal Ball, 102
  The Firefly, 128
  Fountain of Youth, 92
  Justice for Witches, 123
  Lavender Elixir, 84
  Lilith's Power, 120
  The Love Goddess, 43
  The Mermaid, 111
  The NDE, 63
  New Moon, 65
  Pop My Cherry, 48
  The Seductress, 51
  The Spicy Ginger, 113
  Virginal Sacrifice, 132
Blending, 6
Blood Moon, 88

Bourbon
  about, 11
  Divine Feminine, 40
  Lavender Elixir, 84
  The Love Goddess, 43
  The NDE, 63
  The Philosopher's Stone, 119
  Sixth Sense, 107
Brandy
  about, 11
  Crystal Ball, 102
  Full Moon Magic, 59
  Heart Chakra, 53
  Milk Magic, 87
  The Shield, 133
  Sleeping Beauty, 85
  SoulMate, 52
  You've Got Mail, 44
The Brewster, 104

C

Candle magic, 31
The Cauldron, 50
Chamomile, 15
  for hangxiety, 32
  The Night Terror, 121
  Sleeping Beauty, 85
  Stardust, 81
Cherries, 15
  The Coven, 41
  The High Priestess Cosmo, 46
  Justice for Witches, 123
  The Love Goddess, 43
  Midnight Magic, 106
  The Phoenix, 66
  Pop My Cherry, 48
Chocolate, 15
  All Hallows' Eve, 61

Heart Chakra, 53
Cinnamon, 15
  Cinnamon-Rosemary
    Simple Syrup, 20
  Lilith's Power, 120
  Mending Magic Potion, 39
  Milk Magic, 87
  The NDE, 63
  Samhain Spirits, 103
  The Seductress, 51
  Selene's Secret, 105
  The Split, 125
  Summer Solstice (cocktail), 69
  Trial by Fire, 134
Cleansing, 28
Cloves, 15
  Selene's Secret, 105
Cocktail parties
  ending, 32
  holidays, 29–30
  planning, 26–27
  setting up, 27
  spiritually readying home for, 27–28
  welcoming others, 30
Cocktails
  craft, defined, 4–5
  defined, 6
  mixing, 5–6
  step-by-step, 18–19
Cocoa powder, 15
  All Hallows' Eve, 61
  Heart Chakra, 53
Coffee/espresso
  Milk Magic, 87
  The Milky Way, 67
  Samhain Spirits, 103
  The Split, 125

A Witch's Best Friend, 47

Cognac
about, 11
Divine Feminine, 40
The Healer, 90
Trial by Fire, 134
Witch's Wealth, 62

Cola
Eclipse, 64
Justice for Witches, 123
Midnight Magic, 106

Cosmic Cleanse, 94

Cosmic Sigh, 73

The Coven, 41

Covens, 26

Crystal Ball, 102

Crystals, 31

Cucumbers
Cosmic Sigh, 73
Cucumber Charm, 93

Cunningham, Scott, 4

*Cunningham's Encyclopedia
of Wicca in the Kitchen*
(Cunningham), 4

Cupid's Cauldron, 42

D

Dash, 6

Defense against the Dark
Arts, 124

Divine Feminine, 40

Drinkware, 8–9

E

Eclipse, 64

Empath Elixir, 82

Espresso. *See* Coffee/espresso

Eviction Notice, 131

The Evil Eye, 129

F

The Firefly, 128

Floating, 6

Flourishes, 21

Fountain of Youth, 92

Full Moon Magic, 59

G

Garnishes, 14–16

Gin, 71
about, 12
The Amethyst, 91
Autumn Equinox (cocktail), 99
Bewitching Beauty, 86
Blackberry Magic, 126
The Brewster, 104
Cosmic Sigh, 73
The Coven, 41
Full Moon Magic, 59
Hedge Witch, 101
Mending Magic Potion, 39
Sea Witch, 71
The Spicy Ginger, 113
spiritual significance, 7

Ginger
The Guardian, 127
The Spicy Ginger, 113
You've Got Mail, 44

Ginger ale
Full Moon Magic, 59
The Guardian, 127

Ginger beer
The Guardian, 127
Mending Magic Potion, 39

The Spicy Ginger, 113

Glassware, 8–9

The Good Witch, 49

Green Chartreuse

about, 12

Green Witch, 54

Green Witch, 54

Grenadine

Cosmic Cleanse, 94

The Coven, 41

The High Priestess Cosmo, 46

Mercury Retrograde, 60

The Phoenix, 66

Wicked Sexy Witch, 83

Grounding, 28

The Guardian, 127

H

Hadas, Julia Halina, 5

Hangovers, 32

The Healer, 90

Heart Chakra, 53

Hedge Witch, 101

The High Priestess Cosmo, 46

Honey

The Athena, 110

Blackberry Magic, 126

The Cauldron, 50

Crystal Ball, 102

Honey-Lavender Simple
Syrup, 20

Karmic Boost, 114

Lavender Elixir, 84

The Money Maker, 112

The Night Terror, 121

Samhain Spirits, 103

Selene's Secret, 105

Trial by Fire, 134

When Life Gives You Lemons,
Cast a Spell, 74

Horoscopes, 31

Hot drinks

All Hallows' Eve, 61

The Night Terror, 121

Selene's Secret, 105

Sleeping Beauty, 85

Trial by Fire, 134

I

Ice, 14

Infusions, 12–14

Intentions, 5, 7, 17

J

Justice for Witches, 123

K

Karmic Boost, 114

L

Lavender, 15

The Amethyst, 91

Crystal Ball, 102

Empath Elixir, 82

Honey-Lavender Simple
Syrup, 20

Lavender Elixir, 84

The Money Maker, 112

The Night Terror, 121

Sleeping Beauty, 85

Law of Reciprocity, 70

Layering, 6

Lemons, 15

The Amethyst, 91

Autumn Equinox (cocktail), 99

Lemons (*continued*)
  Bewitching Beauty, 86
  Blackberry Magic, 126
  The Cauldron, 50
  Crystal Ball, 102
  Eviction Notice, 131
  The Firefly, 128
  Fountain of Youth, 92
  Full Moon Magic, 59
  The Good Witch, 49
  The High Priestess Cosmo, 46
  Karmic Boost, 114
  Lavender Elixir, 84
  Light & Love, 80
  Mending Magic Potion, 39
  Mystify Me, 109
  The Night Terror, 121
  The Philosopher's Stone, 119
  Repellent, 130
  The Shield, 133
  Sixth Sense, 107
  Trial by Fire, 134
  When Life Gives
    You Lemons, Cast
    a Spell, 74
  You've Got Mail, 44
The Libido, 45
Light & Love, 80
Lilith's Power, 120
Limes, 15
  The Athena, 110
  Cosmic Cleanse, 94
  Cosmic Sigh, 73
  Cupid's Cauldron, 42
  The Firefly, 128
  Fountain of Youth, 92
  The Guardian, 127
  Karmic Boost, 114

Mother Earth, 108
Mystify Me, 109
Protection Potion, 122
SoulMate, 52
Summer Solstice (cocktail), 69
Virginal Sacrifice, 132
Waterworks Martini, 72
Wicked Sexy Witch, 83
Liqueurs
  All Hallows' Eve, 61
  The Brewster, 104
  cream, 12
  Cucumber Charm, 93
  fruit, 12
  The Good Witch, 49
  The Healer, 90
  Heart Chakra, 53
  Hedge Witch, 101
  Mercury Retrograde, 60
  The Milky Way, 67
  Mystify Me, 109
  nut, 12
  The Offering, 70
  Samhain Spirits, 103
  Sea Witch, 71
  The Shield, 133
  Sixth Sense, 107
  The Split, 125
  Strawberry Moon, 68
  A Witch's Best Friend, 47
  Witch's Wealth, 62
Litha, 30
The Love Goddess, 43

M

Mabon, 30
The Magic Wand, 79
Maple syrup

Autumn Equinox (cocktail), 99

The Good Witch, 49

Pop My Cherry, 48

You've Got Mail, 44

Mending Magic Potion, 39

Mercury Retrograde, 60

The Mermaid, 111

Midnight Magic, 106

Miernowska, Marysia, 5

Milk Magic, 87

The Milky Way, 67

Mint, 15

The Amethyst, 91

The Cauldron, 50

Cosmic Sigh, 73

Empath Elixir, 82

Eviction Notice, 131

Fountain of Youth, 92

Green Witch, 54

Karmic Boost, 114

The Mermaid, 111

Mint Simple Syrup, 20

Witch's Wealth, 62

Mixers, 6, 13–14

Mocktails, 18, 30

The Money Maker, 112

Mother Earth, 108

Mystify Me, 109

N

The NDE, 63

Near death experience
(NDE), 63

New Moon, 65

The Night Terror, 121

O

The Offering, 70

Olives, 15

Oranges, 15

The Brewster, 104

The Coven, 41

Karmic Boost, 114

Lilith's Power, 120

The Love Goddess, 43

Mystify Me, 109

The NDE, 63

New Moon, 65

The Offering, 70

The Phoenix, 66

Pop My Cherry, 48

Sea Witch, 71

The Seductress, 51

Selene's Secret, 105

Sixth Sense, 107

You've Got Mail, 44

Ostara, 30

P

Palmieri, Ariana, 73

The Philosopher's
Stone, 119

The Phoenix, 66

Pineapple

The Coven, 41

The Libido, 45

Sun Sacrifice, 100

Virginal Sacrifice, 132

Pomegranate seeds, 16

Mercury Retrograde, 60

Pop My Cherry, 48

Potion brewing, 5, 17, 19

Protection Potion, 122

R

Recipes, about, 22

Repellent, 130

Rituals, 7, 19

Rocks, on the, 6

Rose, 16

  The Good Witch, 49

Rosemary, 16

  Cinnamon-Rosemary

    Simple Syrup, 20

  The Evil Eye, 129

  Hedge Witch, 101

  Lilith's Power, 120

  The Magic Wand, 79

  Mending Magic Potion, 39

  The NDE, 63

  The Seductress, 51

Rum

  about, 12

  Cosmic Cleanse, 94

  The Coven, 41

  Defense against the Dark

    Arts, 124

  Eviction Notice, 131

  Justice for Witches, 123

  The Libido, 45

  Midnight Magic, 106

  Mother Earth, 108

  Mystify Me, 109

  The Offering, 70

  spiritual significance, 7

  Summer Solstice (cocktail), 69

  Sun Sacrifice, 100

S

Sage, 16

  The Athena, 110

  The Healer, 90

  The Offering, 70

  The Shield, 133

  Strawberry Moon, 68

  Waterworks Martini, 72

Samhain Spirits, 103

Schnapps

  about, 12

  The Amethyst, 91

  Sea Witch, 71

Sea Witch, 71

The Seductress, 51

Selene's Secret, 105

Shaking, 6

The Shield, 133

Simple syrups, 20

Sixth Sense, 107

Sleeping Beauty, 85

Smudging, 28

Snacks, 29

SoulMate, 52

Spells, 5, 7, 19

The Spicy Ginger, 113

The Split, 125

Spring Equinox, 30

Stardust, 81

Stirring, 6

Straining, 6

Strawberry Moon, 68

Summer Solstice, 30

Summer Solstice (cocktail), 69

Sun Sacrifice, 100

T

Tarot readings, 31

Tea

  Green Witch, 54

  Mending Magic Potion, 39

  The Night Terror, 121

  Selene's Secret, 105

Tequila

about, 12
The Cauldron, 50
The Firefly, 128
Green Witch, 54
Karmic Boost, 114
Light & Love, 80
The Magic Wand, 79
The Phoenix, 66
SoulMate, 52
Stardust, 81
Thyme, 16
The Magic Wand, 79
The Money Maker, 112
Tools, 10–11
Trial by Fire, 134
Triple sec
The Cauldron, 50
Crystal Ball, 102
The High Priestess
Cosmo, 46
Justice for Witches, 123
Lavender Elixir, 84
The Mermaid, 111
The Philosopher's Stone, 119
Repellent, 130
SoulMate, 52
Sun Sacrifice, 100
You've Got Mail, 44

V

Vanilla beans, 16
Divine Feminine, 40
Stardust, 81
Vanilla Bean Simple
Syrup, 20
Vermouth
The Evil Eye, 129
Full Moon Magic, 59

Waterworks Martini, 72
Virginal Sacrifice, 132
Visualization, 17
Vodka
about, 12
All Hallows' Eve, 61
The Athena, 110
Blood Moon, 88
The Coven, 41
Cucumber Charm, 93
The Evil Eye, 129
Fountain of Youth, 92
Heart Chakra, 53
The High Priestess
Cosmo, 46
Lavender Elixir, 84
Mercury Retrograde, 60
Milk Magic, 87
The Money Maker, 112
The Philosopher's
Stone, 119
Protection Potion, 122
Repellent, 130
The Spicy Ginger, 113
spiritual significance, 7
Strawberry Moon, 68
Waterworks Martini, 72
When Life Gives You Lemons,
Cast a Spell, 74
A Witch's Best Friend, 47

W

Watermelon
Defense against the Dark
Arts, 124
The Mermaid, 111
SoulMate, 52
Waterworks Martini, 72

Waterworks Martini, 72

When Life Gives You Lemons,
    Cast a Spell, 74

Whiskey
  about, 12
  Berry Brew, 89
  Lilith's Power, 120
  The Milky Way, 67
  The Night Terror, 121
  Pop My Cherry, 48
  Samhain Spirits, 103
  The Seductress, 51
  spiritual significance, 7
  The Split, 125
  Wicked Sexy Witch, 83
Wicked Sexy Witch, 83

Wine
  Autumn Equinox (cocktail), 99
  Berry Brew, 89
  Bewitching Beauty, 86
  Blackberry Magic, 126

Eclipse, 64
Empath Elixir, 82
The Good Witch, 49
Mercury Retrograde, 60
The Mermaid, 111
New Moon, 65
sparkling, 12
Winter Solstice, 29

Witchcraft
  alcohol and, 5
  defined, 4
WitchCraft Cocktails
    (Hadas), 5
A Witch's Best Friend, 47
The Witch's Herbal Apothecary
    (Miernowska), 5
Witch's Wealth, 62

Y

You've Got Mail, 44
Yule, 29

Acknowledgments

Thank you to our husbands, Tommy Whalen and Eric Paradis, for expanding our mixology knowledge. We are so grateful for the countless hours they spent crafting magical cocktails with us (and, of course, helping us test and tweak our creations). Then, again, is sampling 80 cocktails *really* a chore?

For the record, we'd also like to give a shout-out to our dear friend and favorite cocktail tester, Il Chy, for sharing his never-ending positive energy and infectious smile.

We so appreciate the *Mystify Me* podcast listeners, whose unending enthusiasm for the cocktails featured in our episodes gave us the confidence to tackle this project.

Last, but certainly not least, we have to thank our spirit posse for guiding us to and through this opportunity—and for flickering the kitchen lights when we needed it most.

About the Authors

Carolyn Wnuk is a practicing clinical therapist and hypnotherapist.
Caroline Paradis is a Reiki master teacher, sound/energy healer, and mindfulness facilitator. When this powerhouse pair teamed up, the explosion of creative energy and ideas ultimately manifested as the *Mystify Me* podcast, which launched in October 2020. This hilarious cocktail hour has become a passion project, a creative outlet, and a platform for demystifying holistic, spiritual, and unconventional practices and topics. So, pull up a seat, grab a cocktail, and join them for an entertaining and mind-bending peek into all things marvelously mystical!

URL/INSTAGRAM: MystifyMePodcast.com/@MystifyMePodcast

LISTEN: Spotify, Apple Podcasts, or wherever you get your podcasts